MW01196315

ACCIDENTALLY
MARRIED

Victorine E. Lieske

Copyright © 2014 by Victorine E. Lieske.

All rights reserved. No part of this publication may be reproduced, distributed or transmitted in any form or by any means, including photocopying, recording, or other electronic or mechanical methods, without the prior written permission of the publisher, except in the case of brief quotations embodied in critical reviews and certain other noncommercial uses permitted by copyright law. For permission requests, write to the publisher, addressed "Attention: Permissions Coordinator," at the address below.

Victorine E. Lieske
PO Box 3
Seward, NE 68434
www.victorinelieske.com

Publisher's Note: This is a work of fiction. Names, characters, places, and incidents are a product of the author's imagination. Locales and public names are sometimes used for atmospheric purposes. Any resemblance to actual people, living or dead, or to businesses, companies, events, institutions, or locales is completely coincidental.

Book Layout ©2014 BookDesignTemplates.com

This book is dedicated to all of the many people who helped shape it into something readable, including all of the wonderful critters over at the Critique Circle. Huge thanks go out to The Local Muse Group, including Lisa Kovanda, Gina Barlean, C.K. Volnek, Kathryn Gilmore, Mary Unger, Dee Feeken Schmidt, Sabrina Sumsion, Brenda Walter, Sydney van ver Heijden, and Belinda Kennington. My thanks also go out to my fine beta readers, Yoly Cortez, Lisa Bjornberg, RJ Licata, Sandy Ewald, Craig Hansen, and Alex Brantham. This book would never have come to pass without help from all of you!

Don't marry the person you think you can live with; marry only the individual you think you can't live without.

–JAMES C. DOBSON

Madison pulled her car into the parking spot, relieved she found an empty space so close to the building. Even though it was only mid-morning, the temperature had risen to an uncomfortable level. A long walk would make her look like a melted ice cube by the time she entered Jameson Technologies. And she couldn't give a bad impression. She needed this job.

Three weeks of handing out résumés and filling out applications, and she hadn't gotten anywhere. She'd promised Carrie she would pay her half of the rent this week, but her bank account was empty.

She shoved the car into park, and it sputtered, choked, and then died. Running the air conditioner always made it feisty. At least the poor thing didn't die on her while driving...most of the time.

She picked up her satchel and stepped out onto the pavement. Heat assaulted her, and she ran a self-conscious hand through her hair. The last few days her horoscope had the theme of something new on her horizon. This was it. Her something new was this job, she was sure of it. She squared her shoulders and tried to put more confidence in her step.

The tallest building in Crimson Ridge stood before her in all its horrific, shiny glory. The impersonal glass reflected the sun into her eyes. The rest of the business district held older buildings with detailed architecture. Jameson Technologies was an eyesore.

As much as she hated the building, she hated mooching off Carrie even more. Her heels clicked on the sidewalk as she neared the glass doors. Her stomach clenched.

Even though she'd never been an administrative assistant, it couldn't be hard. As an actress, she had played several small roles, one of them a secretary. Granted, she had only been on camera for ten seconds before the building blew up, but she had answered the phone and stared at her nails, and she felt like she had embodied the part.

She pulled the smooth metal handle, and the glass door glided open. The lobby felt cold and impersonal with its sleek lines and modern fixtures. Everything was either silver or beige. Down a short hallway to the right, an elevator caught her eye, and a large reception desk sat on the left, which she approached. The woman behind the desk gave a tight-lipped smile.

"May I help you?"

"I'm here to see Mr. Jameson." She tried to sound confident, like she belonged in a place like this.

The woman's eyes traveled the length of her, and she pursed her red lips. "He's been waiting for you."

"He has?" Madison tried to keep her mouth from falling open. When Carrie told her a position at Jameson Technologies was about to open up, she didn't realize her roommate had set up an interview. What luck.

The receptionist nodded, the corners of her mouth pulling down in disapproval. "Go straight up to his office. Twenty-third floor."

Madison strode across the expensive tile floor to the elevator. She pressed the up button and stepped back. Her heart fluttered in her chest. If she played this right, she could be employed by noon.

Carrie was a life saver. Last night she overheard a woman at the shopping center talking about how she was quitting her job. Like a true friend, she asked around until she found out the woman was Mr. Jameson's administrative assistant.

The elevator dinged, and the doors slid open. Madison stepped inside and pressed the button for the twenty-third floor. According to Carrie, the woman indicated she would waltz into Mr. Jameson's office this morning and quit. If the stars aligned, Madison would secure the position before they even called a temp agency.

Her stomach dropped as the elevator lifted and the numbers above the door rose. She smoothed her black skirt and forced herself to think about being an administrative assistant. Answering phones, filing, and...answering phones. Exactly what she was born to do.

The silver doors opened, and she stalked out into another lobby. This one was smaller, but decorated in much the same way. The woman behind the desk reminded her of a bull frog. Large round eyes set wide, a double chin, and a frown that went from one side of her face to the other. A silver name plate revealed her to be Darlene.

For a split second, Madison panicked. What was the assistant still doing here? Carrie made it sound like the woman, Darlene apparently, was going to quit first thing. But her worries fled when Darlene motioned for Madison to pass. "Mr. Jameson wants to speak with you right away."

Darlene must be sticking around to train the next employee. A rush of excitement shot through Madison. That could be her.

She straightened her spine and walked past the desk and entered the office. Huge windows took up the entire east wall, and a fantastic view of the town spread forth. The rest of the spacious office held filing cabinets, an expensive mahogany desk, and some leather chairs. The man behind the desk was much younger than she had imagined the CEO of a large company would be, probably only a year or two her senior. His stormy grey eyes focused on her, and then narrowed.

"You're late." A scowl formed on his face and he stood, his gaze traveling over her. He wore a tie and a white dress shirt, which showed off his muscular physique. His jet black hair was neatly styled, probably some kind of corporate cut.

Confidence, she reminded herself.

Madison crossed the room and extended her hand. "I'm sorry, Mr. Jameson, I was not aware Carrie had set up—"

"And what are you wearing? You look like you're going to a business meeting." His scowl deepened, which she thought wasn't possible.

"I uh—"

"Never mind. You'll do." He grabbed a briefcase from the floor and strode across the room, past her, and out the door, which he left open.

Madison stared after him. What happened? *You'll do?* What did that mean?

He stuck his head back into the office. "You want the job, or what?"

Her pulse raced. She got the job! "Yes, sir!"

"Come on, then." He motioned with his head.

She jumped into motion, following him until he stopped at the elevator. He must want to give her a tour of the place. Unnecessary, but it didn't matter, she got the job. She felt like doing a little leprechaun dance, but settled for a satisfied smile.

They stepped into the elevator, and she became aware of their close proximity. Masculinity rolled off him. He smelled of aftershave and expensive soap, and she had to step back in order to clear her head. He was her boss. She couldn't think of him as anything else.

He pressed the button marked B2. He must want to show her everything, from the basement up. She shrugged. Okay. After they descended, the doors opened and Mr. Jameson disappeared into the parking garage.

Warning bells sounded in Madison's head. What was going on here?

"Come on," he called, his voice echoing through the dim space. "We're already late."

She stuck her head out of the elevator and spotted him stalking toward a black luxury car. It beeped and the doors unlocked. "Wait...I—"

"What? Are you having second thoughts?" He stopped and glared at her. "I don't have time for this. I'll double your pay. A thousand dollars for a few hours of your time."

Alarm rang through her. What kind of job was this? She gripped the elevator door jam, keeping the doors open. "I think there's been some kind of—"

His phone rang and he held up his hand to silence her. "Yeah?"

He opened his trunk and slung his briefcase into the back. "Wait, what?" His piercing gaze traveled over to her and froze. "Okay. Thanks for calling." He jammed his finger on his phone to hang up, then he slipped it into his pocket.

"You're not Nathan's cousin." His glare was accusing, and he folded his arms across his chest.

She shook her head, confused.

"Who are you?" he demanded.

"Madison Nichols. I've come to apply for the administrative assistant position that recently became available." Her voice sounded paper thin to her ears.

Mr. Jameson's shoulders slumped and one corner of his mouth twitched. "I'm sorry. I've made a terrible mistake."

"I'll say," she mumbled.

He started toward her but stopped when she shrank back. "Listen, I've got to go to a family function this evening, and it would ease the tension if I brought a date."

It was Madison's turn to narrow her eyes. He was going to pay someone to date him? Who does that?

He stuffed his hands in his pockets. "Sounds weird, but I'm not really the dating type, so I was going to hire someone." Color touched his cheeks. At least he had the good sense to look embarrassed.

When she didn't speak, he continued. "That was Nathan on the phone. His cousin is sick...so I'm left without a date."

She glared at him. What exactly was he asking her to do? "I'm here to apply for the *administrative assistant* position," she repeated.

He clenched his jaw. "I have no *administrative assistant* positions open at this time."

Heat rose to her face. The jerk. "So, now there is no job unless I agree to be your paid escort?" Her voice rose in pitch.

He sighed. "It's only a family dinner. My father's birthday. And it's more like an acting job than anything."

Her head snapped up. How did he know she was an actress?

Mr. Jameson took a step closer. "A thousand dollars, and all you have to do is eat my stepmother's cooking, laugh at my father's lame jokes, and act like you don't hate me. That's it. I swear."

"Where does your family live?"

"Highland Falls. It's a three-hour drive. We'll get there around..." He checked his watch. "One-thirty. We spend some time with the family, eat dinner, and leave. I'll have you back here by ten at the latest."

She eyeballed him. He didn't look like he was lying. With his clean-shaven face and well manicured nails, he appeared quite sophisticated. Was she really considering this? A thousand dollars would pay her half of the rent for a couple of months. She really needed the money. "And if I agree, maybe an administrative assistant job would become available?"

He frowned, scrubbed his hand over his chin, and squinted at her. "Maybe."

"Deal." Did she say yes? She must be out of her mind.

A smug look flashed across his face before he opened the driver's side door and slid onto the seat. "Well come on, then. We're late."

How rude. This guy was something else. He didn't even open her car door for her. But she figured she could ignore his rude behavior if it meant paying the rent.

She left the protection of the elevator doorway, which caused the doors to swish shut as if angry at being held open for so long. The sound of her heels on the cement echoed through the parking garage. She yanked open the passenger door and plopped down, hugging her satchel to her chest.

He scowled at her for a second. "Toss it in the back."

As they drove, Madison figured out why they called them luxury cars. The plush seat molded to her body, the ride smooth and quiet. Mr. Jameson even seemed to relax a bit.

"There are a few things you should know, in order to play this part correctly. First, we've been dating for four months."

Madison turned to him, forcing herself not to make a face. That's why he needed a date so bad. He'd lied to his family. And now they were demanding to see his mystery girlfriend. She pursed her lips.

"We've been to the opera, the ballet, and we frequent the art museum."

What kind of a person lies to their family? Her opinion of him dropped. "Uh huh." She nodded.

"You're refined, so it's important you act the part."

Did he just call her unrefined? What a colossal jerk. She narrowed her eyes. "Sure."

"We are on the verge of being serious, but don't worry, I won't have to see the family again until Christmas, and by then we'll have broken up." He gripped the steering wheel and glanced at her. "Got all that?"

What did he think she was, an idiot? It's not like he was teaching her trigonometry. "Dating for four months...refined...and on the verge of a break up. Got it."

He grimaced. "You don't have to think about the break up. That won't happen for a few months."

She lifted an eyebrow. "I should portray a hint of discord between us, so when you eventually tell them, it seems more believable, don't you think?"

He signaled and changed lanes to pass a slow moving semi truck. "I suppose."

Madison closed her eyes for a moment, trying to get into her part. She imagined herself being a woman who liked the finer things in life. Someone who would date a wealthy CEO like Mr. Jameson. Her eyes snapped open. "What's your name? I can't really call you Mr. Jameson in front of your family."

"Jared."

The name fit him somehow. A power name. Muscular. She shook her head. She shouldn't be thinking about his muscles. "How did we meet?"

His jaw muscles twitched. "I didn't tell them how we met, so it's irrelevant."

"What if someone asks?"

"No one will ask. And if they do, make something up. It doesn't matter." He stared straight ahead.

Madison fiddled with her fingers. He wasn't very friendly, was he? She could see now why he had to pay someone to go out with him. If this was how he treated women, he'd be alone the rest of his life. Even with his handsome face. It's what's inside that truly attracts.

She wondered if he was always this uptight. There had to be something she could say to make him loosen up, or this would be a very long evening. "Since I might be working at Jameson Technologies, why don't you tell me a little bit about your company?"

"We design and build technology like semiconductors and virtual memory, and we invest in other innovative companies." The corner of his mouth lifted a little. Not a full smile, but she decided it was progress.

"And Darlene, how long was she working as your administrative assistant before she handed in her resignation?"

His eyebrows raised and he jerked his head in her direction. "What?"

Her face grew warm and she shifted uncomfortably in her seat. Darlene had not quit yet. Great. Now what was she supposed to do? "Um, a friend of mine overheard Darlene talking. She said she was going to quit her job today. Sorry to break it to you. I guess she hasn't done it yet."

Deep laughter bubbled up from his chest, and he smiled – an actual real smile. He continued to chuckle while swerving into the other lane to pass another car.

She couldn't fathom why he was laughing. Losing an employee was not humorous. She had a sneaking suspicion he was laughing at her. "What's so funny?" she snapped.

"Darlene threatens to quit three times a week. Never actually follows through."

Anger festered in her like an ulcer. Jared had no intention of hiring her. "I guess there's no position for me at your company." The words came out clipped.

Jared stopped laughing and grew serious. "I said *maybe*. I didn't say *yes*."

Madison clenched her fists, her fingernails digging into her skin. "And because you wanted me to pretend to be your girlfriend, you lied."

"You're overreacting."

Maybe she was. But he had lied, and she wasn't going to let him get away with it. "You knew I wanted a job."

"I'm giving you a job. What's the matter with you?"

The condescending way he said it made her blood boil. He had manipulated her into doing this. She suddenly felt cheap. Used. And cruising down the interstate miles away from home, there was nothing she could do about it.

She folded her arms across her chest and glared at him. If he wanted her to play a part for his family, she sure would.

But maybe not the *refined* girlfriend he was hoping for.

2

Jared's stomach tightened as he drove down the winding street to his childhood home. Being in Highland Falls always brought back the painful past. He never seemed to move beyond it.

Madison sat with her hands folded in her lap, silently staring out the window. Her blonde hair brushed her shoulders. Her legs, long and shapely, crossed at the ankles. She was going to be perfect. She really fit the part. If only she hadn't worn a cheap business suit.

He shook his head. It didn't matter. His family wouldn't think much of it. They'd probably assume she came right from work.

The twisty street threaded past large homes with lush green lawns. This was country club territory, the kind of people who cared about appearances and kept their problems locked safely away in the liquor cabinet.

He pulled into the long circular driveway and stopped the car. As soon as he cut the engine, Madison hopped out. He hurried around to her side. "You should have let me open your door."

Madison frowned. "Why?"

"It's the proper thing to do."

"Then why didn't you open my car door in the parking garage? Or is it only the proper thing to do when someone might be watching?"

He rolled his eyes and started up the sidewalk. No use in arguing with her. She was a temp. Someone to play a part to ease the constant hounding. And he was pretty sure no one was at the window.

They approached his father's sandstone house. Not quite large enough to be called a mansion, and yet pretentious enough to impress the Joneses. A stone lion sat on either side of the concrete stairs. They always made Jared feel like he lived at a library.

He pressed the bell and Irene, his father's wife of the month, opened the door. Her long black hair was pulled back in a bun, a couple of chopsticks sticking out of it. She wore a tank top and capris.

"Jared!" She donned her fake smile and ushered them inside. "Please come in."

"Madison, this is my stepmother, Irene. Irene, this is Madison."

Madison whacked him in the chest. "Stepmother? Get out! I thought she was your sister."

He stared at her. What was she doing? But the comment obviously pleased Irene, for she laughed her little twitter of a giggle and took Madison into an embrace.

"Aren't you a dear? Come meet the rest of the family. They're already here."

Of course. She had to get a little dig in that he was late. He clenched his jaw and followed her through the kitchen to the family room.

When they entered, everyone stopped talking and turned to stare. His gaze landed on Shelly, his aunt, who had been the only constant mother figure in his life since his mother died. Her unnaturally pale face made it obvious her condition was taking a toll on her. His chest squeezed. She was the only reason he came to family events. How many more would she be around for?

Irene put her arm around Madison. "Everyone, this is Madison, Jared's girlfriend." She pointed around the room. "That's Mark, Zachary, and Patricia, Shelly, and of course, Maxwell, Jared's father. But don't worry about remembering names, you'll pick it up. Would you like to sit down while I get you something to drink?"

Madison looked at Jared sideways, and for a second he saw something gleam in her eye. Something almost devilish. Then it vanished. She faced Irene and smiled. "I'd love a drink. Do you have any vodka?"

Jared's mouth went dry. Was she nuts? He stared at her bright grin and realization crashed down on him. This was on purpose. Payback for saying there might be a position open at his company.

This was going to be a long day.

Irene laughed again. "We have ice water, Coke and tea."

"Coke is fine, although if you dump a little vodka in it I won't be disappointed." She winked at Irene and took the three steps down into the family room. She plopped down on the sectional and patted the seat next to her. "Come on, sweetie."

All eyes turned to him. After he hugged Shelly and said a quick 'happy birthday' to his father, he sat beside her.

Patricia, his cousin, smiled at him. Her blonde hair was cut in a pixie style, much shorter than the last time he'd seen her. "We're so happy you came, Jared. And it's nice to meet your girl-friend."

"I'm glad Jared brought me. I mean, I'll bet you were all starting to think Jared here made me up." Madison slapped him on the leg.

Hard.

Everyone laughed as heat rose to his face. He pushed down the urge to fire off a retort. She was baiting him. Trying to get under his skin. Instead, he focused on his family. Patricia and Zachary were getting really chummy. She was practically sitting on his lap. It wouldn't be long before they were making an announcement. Luckily, his father seemed to be the only one in the family with the propensity to exchange his spouse for a new model each year. He'd lost count as to how many ex-wives his father had. His mother was the only one who mattered to him, and she'd died long ago.

Patricia leaned forward. "Tell us about your-self, Madison. Jared's been so evasive."

Madison patted Jared on the leg. "He's so cute. He doesn't like to talk about himself."

Mark snorted. "He doesn't like to talk at all."

His half-brother from wife number three, Mark had never grown close to Jared. Most of Jared's time growing up was spent with his cousin, Patricia. The only time he saw Mark was for a few weeks each summer.

Patricia threw a dirty look at Mark. "What do you do, Madison?"

"I'm an actress." She glanced at Jared, prob-ably to gauge his reaction. He kept his face straight, intent on not giving her what she wanted.

"That's so cool. Have you been in any mov-ies?" Patricia's eyes glinted. She was the kind of person who liked everyone, and they all liked her. Perpetually happy, that's what he used to call her.

"I was an extra in *Big Fat Liar.*"

The comment caught him off guard and he coughed. He had to admit, she was quick on her feet. If her barbs weren't pointed at him, he might enjoy her wit.

"And I played the administrative assistant in *The Sixteenth Floor*."

Patricia's eyes widened. "The movie that came out last year? Are you serious?"

Madison nodded. "It was a small part, but I did have a short speaking line."

"Get out of here. Now I have to watch it again."

"I have the DVD," his father said, reaching behind to the cabinet.

Patricia clapped her hands together. "Oh, let's watch your scene. Shall we?"

"I'm about twenty minutes into the movie." She appeared to be enjoying the attention.

He leaned over and whispered in her ear. "Wait, you really were in *The Sixteenth Floor?*"

She glared at him. "Yes. What did you think, I was going to *lie* about it?"

He shrugged and let it go. The family members crowded around to see the television screen while his father inserted the disc. Irene entered the room, handed Madison a Coke, and sat next to his father.

Everyone seemed impressed with her part, even though she was only on camera for a few seconds. "Nice," Mark said, which was high praise coming from him. Even Jared reluctantly agreed she looked good on camera.

Zachary put his arm around Patricia. "How did you two meet?"

Madison gave Jared a sideways glance, the corner of her mouth curled up, and he knew something terrible was coming. Time slowed down. The hairs on the back of his neck stood. It was like he was watching two cars heading for each other and had no power to stop either one. The only thing he could do was watch the crash happen.

Madison smiled at Zachary. "I'm so glad you asked. This is a great story."

Thinking maybe he could save himself from the wreck, he jumped in. "We met at the opera."

"Yes," she said, and her smile widened. "In the women's bathroom."

A few mouths dropped open and Mark choked on his soda. Jared knew he had to salvage this quickly. "Well, not really *inside* the women's bathroom. We met in the hallway."

She patted him on the leg. "Jared here doesn't quite remember, since he was a bit tipsy at the time, but it definitely was *inside* the women's restroom. He came stumbling in and ran right into me. Of course, I was startled to say the least, I mean, a man in the women's bathroom! But he looked so cute with a little bit of drool running down his chin—"

"I was not slobbering drunk." He didn't mean to yell, but it came out a bit loud. Heat crept up his neck, and he loosened his tie.

"Oh, no, dear. I said tipsy. Anyway, I helped him out to his car, and we got to talking. Turns out he needed an administrative assistant at Jameson Technologies so he hired me on the spot."

Was she trying to blackmail him into a job? She had some nerve.

There was no way he was going to spend another second with her after today, much less hire her for anything. He shifted in his seat. "Unfortunately, she couldn't do the job well enough, so I had to fire her."

Patricia drew in a sharp breath, and everyone stared at him like he confessed to eating children for breakfast.

Madison glared at him. "But he did offer me a second job—"

"Which she refused, of course, since I had just fired her. She holds grudges. Big, big grudges."

"And don't you think I deserved to hold a grudge after being treated like that?" Her cheeks were flushed, and her back straight.

He put his arm around her. "Of course, everything was smoothed over after we started dating and fell for each other. The end. That's how we met." He pasted on a smile and she mimicked the expression.

Patricia's eyes were about as big as he'd ever seen them. "Wow, I can't believe you agreed to go out with him after what he did."

"It didn't happen right away. He kept asking, begging really, and I kept saying no. Then one day he came to my apartment and serenaded me from outside on the lawn."

Begging? Serenading? Jared couldn't believe what he was hearing. Shelly put a proud smile on her face that seemed to say, *I knew you were romantic deep inside.*

Patricia put her hand over her heart. "Awe, that's the sweetest thing I've ever heard Jared doing. In fact, that's so unlike him. He must be really smitten with you."

Madison patted him on the cheek. "It was adorable. I can still see him out there, holding a single rose, kneeling in the grass, and belting out *Hopelessly Devoted to You.*"

Patricia, Shelly and Irene were obviously pleased. The guys were all looking at him like he'd put on a dress. Jared pushed down the urge to run from the room.

His father frowned. "Jared can sing?"

"Not really. It was totally off-key. The neighbors opened their windows and cursed. A dog started whimpering. I think someone threw a tomato. But it melted my heart."

"That's so romantic." Irene frowned at her husband. "That definitely doesn't run in the family."

Madison raised an eyebrow, and a devilish look flashed across her face again. "You should hear what he did for my birthday."

Jared stood. "I think they've heard enough for now, sweetie. And I'm ready for a snack. Anyone else? I think I saw Irene putting out some cheese and crackers."

"I was about to invite people to go fill up a plate." Irene motioned toward the other room. "Dinner will be a while, and I don't want anyone going hungry."

As his family stood and made their way to the table, Jared glanced back at Madison's face. Disappointment flitted across for a second, but then she recovered and hopped off the couch.

"Great. Then maybe Jared can share our big announcement."

Everyone stopped and all eyes landed on him.

3

Madison knew she was pushing things too far, but she couldn't stop herself. She was having way too much fun. The looks Jared was giving her were priceless. She almost broke character and busted out laughing at his expression when she told everyone they met in the women's bathroom. And now he gawked at her, mouth open like a cod fish, eyes bugged out...she wished there was a hidden camera.

He coughed into his fist. "It's not an announcement. I mean, there is no announcement.

There's nothing. We're just normal." He waved his arm in a lame 'nothing to see here' gesture.

She held in a giggle. He was so cute when he was caught off guard. Much better than the corporate grump she'd met earlier. With his tie loose and hair slightly rumpled, he was actually sexy. It didn't hurt that he had broad, muscular shoulders and a trim waist. She shook the thought out of her head. She couldn't go soft on him. He hadn't paid enough yet for being such a jerk.

"Oh, I'm sorry, darling. Did I spoil the surprise?" She crossed the room and put her arms around his neck. "Jared asked me to marry him."

Patricia squealed and ran over, throwing her arms around them. "I can't believe it!"

Jared's face paled. "But you said no." He stepped back from her. "She said no," he said louder. "So, that's it."

Patricia stepped back, confusion on her face.

"Oh, sweetie, I didn't say *no*, I said *let me think about it*. And I've thought about it...and my answer is yes! We're getting married!" She pulled Jared and Patricia back into a hug.

The room filled with instant conversation. The women hugged Madison while the men congratulated Jared. Shelly was so happy she had tears in her eyes, which brought instant guilt. She hadn't thought about the consequences of her rash decision to announce an engagement. Seeing Shelly so moved made her realize these people were real, and she was lying to them.

The thought made her pause. Had she made a mistake? Shelly smiled through her tears and whispered, "Congratulations."

Maybe she had taken things too far, but everything would be resolved soon. Their pretend engagement would become a pretend breakup. His family might be a bit disappointed, but they really didn't know her very well. How upset could they be? Besides, it was all Jared's fault for lying in the first place.

Irene squeezed her hands. "This is wonderful news. We're so happy for you."

Jared's father pulled her into a tight embrace. He was a retired prosecuting attorney and he looked the part. Graying hair and the kind of body that used to be muscular but whose pot belly had taken over a few years ago. His face had a bit of a bulldog look to it. Sagging cheeks and a wide chin. "How did you hook him? I thought Jared would remain a bachelor the rest of his life." Madison shrugged and laughed off his comment.

Patricia flitted around the room, her hands covering her mouth. "I can't believe this." Her eyes misted over. "We were going to wait until dinner, but now...well, Zachary has proposed to me, too!"

The room erupted once again. More congratulations and hugs were exchanged. Shelly cried again. Then Patricia turned to Madison, her eyes wide. "Oh my gosh, I didn't mean to destroy your moment. I'm so sorry!"

Guilt once again plagued Madison. "No, this is wonderful. You didn't ruin anything. I'm thrilled for you."

Patricia's face lit up. "You're the sweetest thing. I know we're going to be close. Like sisters." Her face held a child-like innocence, large eyes and flawless skin. Madison couldn't help but like her.

"I have the best idea." Patricia grabbed Madison's arm. "We should have a double wedding!" She squealed, then turned to Zachary for approval.

Her fiancé, the handsome laid back kind of guy, nodded and lifted his shoulders. "Whatever you want, honey."

Madison's head began to spin. Patricia looked so happy. How could she say no? "Sure. A double wedding would be great."

Jared's face turned red. He grabbed her arm in a vice grip and whispered, "We need to talk." And then louder he said, "Excuse us for a second."

He pulled her into a spare bedroom, shut the door and then rounded on her. "Have you lost your mind?"

Madison had never heard anyone quiet-shout before. "Hey, you're the one who wanted me to lie. I'm just making it more interesting."

"This isn't a game." He ground his teeth.

"You're the one who made it a game when you brought me here to pretend—"

"I only wanted you to be nice and eat dinner." The quiet was diminishing and the shout taking over. "How could you do this?"

His anger rolled off him in waves. Before she thought about what she was doing, she put her hands on his chest. His muscles tensed.

"Relax. Tomorrow you can tell them we got into a fight and the wedding is off."

He stepped back, breaking the contact. "You don't know what you've done."

His attitude was beginning to irk her. "What?" she snapped.

"My aunt Shelly...she's sick. All she's been talking about for the past five years is how I need to find someone to marry before she dies. A double wedding? Can't you see? That's exactly what she wants. And you're giving it to her...only to tear it out of her hands again."

A dull pain started in her chest and her throat tightened. "Well, maybe she won't be so upset when we break up, because she'll have Patricia's wedding. Right?"

Jared swallowed and his eyes bore into hers. "You'd better hope that's how it goes down. Because the last thing I'm going to do is break her heart."

She wrung her hands. This was not going as planned. She wasn't doing this to hurt his family. If only his aunt didn't want them to get married. A thought struck her. It was kind of far fetched, but it might work. "I know what to do. We'll get her to suggest the marriage might not be the best idea." She poked him in the chest for emphasis, which was kind of like poking a bear, and she tucked her hands behind her back hoping he hadn't noticed.

The corners of his mouth pulled down. "How do you propose we do that?"

"We make her think I'm not suited for you." Scenarios filled her head and she began to pace the room. "I've already acted a bit...raw."

Jared snorted. "Yeah. Raw. That's one way to say it."

She ignored him. "I can amp it up a bit. Make her think we'd never work as a couple. With your personality, this should be easy."

"What do you mean by that?"

"Calm down. It's not an insult. I'm just saying you're a little...stiff."

He raised an eyebrow. "That's not an insult?"

She stopped pacing, her high heels making her feet hurt. "No. You corporate people can't have personalities getting in the way of your money making and things." The words weren't coming out right, and she blew out a frustrated breath.

A twitch in his lip told her he was trying not to smile. "I see."

"Never mind. Let's go out there and force your family to break us up." She plastered on a happy face and dragged him out of the room.

Madison tugged Jared into the kitchen where his family was gathered. An island held trays of vegetables, cheese, crackers and dip. A stack of small plates sat on the granite counter top.

She made a show of picking up a dish and looking at it. "Can I have a bigger plate? I'm starving."

Irene patted her back. "Of course, honey." She crossed the kitchen and opened a cabinet door.

"Never mind. I'll just use this." Madison picked up the serving tray filled with cheese. She slid onto the bar stool next to Jared. His lip twitched.

"My, you're hungry. No problem. I'll get some more." Irene fussed in the cupboards and pulled out another tray, and then started slicing cheese.

No one said anything, but Madison caught a few strange looks.

Shelly turned to her. "How did you get a part in a movie from here in the Midwest?" She sat perched on a bar stool, her legs crossed and her hands on her knee. She did look thin and pale. Under her makeup, her cheeks were gaunt. Guilt wormed its way through Madison.

"I was living in Hollywood when I got the acting gigs." She stuffed a few pieces of cheese in her mouth.

"What brought you to Nebraska?"

She chewed the wad of cheese and swallowed. "I ran out of money, and wasn't earning enough from my acting to stay in Hollywood, so I moved back in with my college roommate." Unfortunately she didn't have to lie to look lame, she was doing a great job being pathetic on her own.

Shelly's eyebrows rose. "What do you do now?"

Good question. She had no idea. Her plans were to get a job, save up more money and maybe try out for a few local productions. She hadn't thought much ahead of that. "I'm kind of in between things right now." And just to spice things up, she said, "I've been thinking of trying street performance."

Patricia's mouth dropped open. This was it. The moment when Jared's family realized she was a flake and not worthy of his affections.

But instead of a look of disdain, Patricia smiled and clasped her hands together. "Zachary was in a small vocal group back in college and they performed on the streets of New York. They raked it in. It paid for half his tuition!"

"Oh, I love street performers." Irene patted her hair and got a faraway look on her face.

So much for that. But she wasn't ready to give up yet. "I don't sing. But did learn how to play the recorder in 3rd grade." She flashed her best dumb blonde smile.

Jared's lip did another twitching thing, and he coughed into his fist.

Irene's laughter bubbled up. "You're so funny." Then she turned. "Jared, she's a keeper. Don't let go of this one." She patted his hand.

Great. That didn't work at all. She stared at their faces, all smiling at her. What was wrong with them? Couldn't they see she was off her rocker? His family was too accepting. What could she do to make them not like her?

She stole a glance at Jared. The smirk was gone, and his cheeks were pink. "No, she's serious. She wants to play the recorder...professionally."

Irritation ran through Madison. There was Mr. CEO, trying to take over the situation.

Oh, heavens, he's still talking.

"In fact, she told me she was trying to learn to play the recorder with her feet. Right, honey?"

Madison narrowed her eyes at him. "Yes, but I gave up on that. Don't you remember? It was the day you baked me a three-layer cake. You remember, sugar plum...the one you frosted in white and then added the little red roses on top?"

Everyone stared, their eyes wide.

Patricia giggled. "Jared baked a cake for you? Now that's something I'd like to see."

Jared glared at her. "Oh, sure, I remember. That was the day you decided to practice your yoga positions and you somehow managed to fling yourself out the window."

Shelly gasped.

"It was a ground floor window, and it really was more of a patio door thing, so I wasn't hurt. Which is funny, because Jared ran outside to see if I was okay, forgetting he had my frilly apron on. The neighbors kind of look at him strangely now."

The kitchen erupted in laughter. Jared's face turned dark red. Then purple. He folded his arms across his chest. "At least I was wearing pants."

Heat crept up her neck as more laughter filled the room. "I had my workout shorts on."

"I'm not sure you can call those shorts."

"They're a little skimpy, but you've got me beat when you wear your tiny pink Speedos."

Jared's face darkened again, a shade somewhere between 'You're in big trouble' and 'I'm gonna kill you.'

"I do believe you gave me those Speedos, and I don't think I've ever worn them."

Irene came up behind them and put her arms around them. "You two sound like an old married couple already."

As the evening progressed, Madison came to the conclusion she liked Jared's family, more than she intended to. His father was pretty quiet most of the time. For a retired prosecuting attorney, he had more bark than bite. A distinguished air hung about him.

Shelly seemed to be the glue that held the family together. She was the typical mother figure, even though she was technically Jared's aunt. When tempers flared, she was there to smooth things over.

Irene was a bit flighty, although very nice. Madison was surprised to learn she had been married to Maxwell for only ten months.

There was obvious tension between Mark and Jared. Maybe half-sibling rivalry. She wasn't sure. They kept tossing glares and snide remarks at each other. Mark actually looked a lot like Jared. His eyes were more of an almond shape, but the half-brothers shared the same dark hair and high cheek bones.

Zachary and Patricia were the perfect young couple in love. Patricia positively radiated. She was chatty and likable, and laughed easily. Zachary was quiet, and maybe a bit shy in front of her family. He managed one of the stores in his family's hardware business.

Madison enjoyed talking with and getting to know Jared's family. Everyone seemed relaxed and happy...even Jared mellowed out. At least he wasn't scowling anymore.

Patricia pulled out her engagement ring and everyone oohed and ahhed appropriately. The diamond was huge. Probably set Zachary back quite a bit.

"Where's Madison's ring?" Patricia asked, poking Jared in the side.

His eyes widened. He stammered a minute, before Madison took pity on him and said, "We've been to the jewelry store several times, but I haven't found anything I like. I'm picky that way."

He nodded, his face relaxing. "Yep. We haven't found the right one."

"Ooh, you should go to the little shop on First and Pine. It has amazing hand-crafted rings. I'm sure Madison will like something there."

Madison could tell what was going through his mind, as his mouth opened and closed. She could almost see green dollar signs shining in his eyes. She decided to save him again. "I have really simple tastes. In fact, I may wear my great-grandmother's ring."

"Oh, a family heirloom! That would be so meaningful." Patricia clasped Zachary's hand. "And romantic."

Mark ran his hand through his dark hair. "Wouldn't it be more romantic if it was Jared's family heirloom?"

Patricia scowled at him. "Hush."

"Just sayin..."

"You be nice," Patricia scolded.

"But it's her own ring. That's all I'm sayin'."

"I'm taking her ring-shopping tomorrow." Jared cleared his throat and tugged at his tie. "I mean, there was one shop down the street from my company that we haven't tried yet. It's been closed for remodeling. We're going tomorrow."

"Wonderful," Shelly said.

"My jeweler can get you a good deal." Maxwell put his arm around Irene. "You'd never believe the price he gave me on the one I bought Irene."

"Only because you buy them in bulk," Jared muttered.

Madison's mouth dropped. Luckily, no one else heard the comment.

She forgot about acting uncouth in front of his family as the time wore on. When it came time for dinner, they moved into the formal dining room. A long oak table, lavishly decorated with candles and beautiful white china, sat in the middle of the room. A roast on a silver platter took the center spot on the table. Wine glasses, polished silverware…and the cloth napkins were folded in fancy shapes. Madison half expected to see a butler waltz in with a tux and little white towel draped over one arm. They seated the happy couples next to each other on one side, across from Mark, Shelly and Irene. Maxwell, sitting at the head of the table, said grace.

Shelly stood and raised her wine glass, tapping it with her knife. "I'd like to offer a toast, to my brother." She turned to Maxwell, who had a grin on his face. "You're another year older, but we all know you're no wiser." A few chuckles sounded. "But we love you, anyway. May this year be as wonderful as the last one. And may your new bride be around at least for your next birthday."

Laughter filled the room. Even Irene giggled. Madison turned to Jared. He sat with his back straight, his jaw clenched. When everyone raised their glass, he didn't move. Madison nudged him and he reluctantly followed suit.

"To Maxwell," Patricia said, a bright smile on her face. Either she was oblivious to the tension, or she was ignoring it.

The food looked delicious, and Madison plopped a healthy helping of mashed potatoes on her plate. Jared stared at her and then gave her a slight head shake. She frowned. Who cared if his family thought she was a pig? Or was he trying to tell her she should watch her weight? What a jerk. She raised her chin and added another spoonful. They were loaded potatoes, with chunks of bacon and chives in them. Her mouth watered.

When her plate was full, she glanced around the table. Most everyone else had conservative portions, similar to Jared's plate. Maybe it was a rich people thing. Smaller portions to fit in to those designer jeans. She mentally shrugged. No reason to go hungry. After all, she was trying to make his family think she didn't belong.

Jared seemed particularly interested in her plate. He wouldn't stop staring at it. She took a hearty scoop of potatoes and shoved them into her mouth.

The first thing she noticed was the temperature. The potatoes were cold. Then the taste hit her. What was that? They tasted like dirty dish water! And those chunks were not bacon bits. She didn't know what they were. She forced her jaw to chew, hoping the warmth of her mouth would make the potatoes tolerable enough to swallow.

As she worked on getting the food to go down, she noticed the corner of Jared's mouth twitching. He turned away, but then his shoulders started shaking. The scoundrel was laughing at her.

She kicked him under the table, and he turned to her, a full-fledged smile on his face. Such a rare occurrence, she'd noticed, but when it did happen, he looked like a model. A hint of blue infected his steel-grey eyes, and his long eyelashes made him even sexier. Her stomach plummeted to her knees. If Jared made an effort, he could have any girl on his arm.

Madison forced the chunky, cold potatoes down and held back a giggle, unable to be mad. He *had* tried to warn her. He picked up his napkin and wiped his face to hide his laughter, a chuckle escaping. She pinched her lips together, desperately trying not to laugh, but that only made it erupt in a forceful "Ha!"

She clamped her hand over her mouth.

Patricia's eyes were full of mirth. "Looks like Jared and Madison have some kind of inside joke going."

Mark frowned. "Since when does Jared laugh at jokes?"

Shelly patted Mark's hand. "He's in love. That tends to change everything."

Jared swallowed his laughter and put his arm around Madison. "Yes. Love. That's it." He looked down at her, a hint of a smile on his face.

Her skin tingled where he touched her, and she gazed up into his eyes. "Yep. We're in love."

As the attention of the family drifted to other things, Madison tentatively took a nibble from the roast. At least that was decent. It was hard to mess up a roast, she supposed. The vegetables, on the other hand, were half frozen, and the side salad had a weird taste to it. She stuck with the meat, and pushed the rest of the food around her plate until everyone was done.

After the dishes were scraped and in the dishwasher, everyone gathered back in the family room to watch Maxwell open his birthday gifts. Madison had not seen Jared with a gift, and she hoped he brought something. Her instinct told her he hadn't, which would embarrass her. She sat next to Jared on the couch, hoping he had done something for his father's birthday.

Irene brought out a stack of brightly wrapped gifts. Jared reached into his pocket and placed an envelope on top. It turned out to be a gift card. Pretty lame, in Madison's opinion, but at least he'd gotten something.

After the gift unwrapping, Shelly pulled out a camera and announced, "Photo time! I have to get pictures of the two newly engaged couples."

She turned to Patricia and Zachary first, snapping some great pictures of them posing and goofing around. They made a wonderful couple. When they looked at each other, their eyes shone. Madison's stomach tightened. She and Jared could never look like them. Surely everyone would see they were a fraud.

Shelly turned the camera on them. "Your turn." The camera clicked a couple of times, then she added, "Just act natural."

They sat on the couch, Jared's back stiff, his hands folded in his lap. At least he plastered on a fake smile.

"Relax a bit. You look like you're posing for a mug shot. Jared, put your arm around your fiancée." Shelly adjusted the camera settings and snapped a couple more photos.

"That's a little better. Now I want an action shot. Give her a kiss."

Madison looked up at Jared, and he leaned over and gave her a quick peck on the cheek.

Shelly laughed. "Oh, you can do better than that, hon. Kiss her like you mean it."

Jared shot Madison an apologetic look, which actually was quite sweet of him. She didn't care if he kissed her. She was an actress, after all. Kissing on set was no big deal.

He leaned in and brushed his lips over hers. A light, innocent gesture. At least that's how it started out, until he deepened the kiss. Her heart raced and her mind went blank. Time slowed as the sensation of his soft lips touching hers sent ripples of pleasure across her skin. His hand cradled the back of her head, pulling her closer.

The smell of his cologne mixed with his masculinity heightened her senses. Before she knew what she was doing her arms were around his neck, and she was kissing him back. Warmth spread through her as his gentle touch sent tingles down her spine.

He pulled back, ending the kiss and staring at her, his eyebrows knit together. The room erupted in cat calls and hoots. Madison's cheeks heated. She'd forgotten where they were.

"Now that's how it's done." Maxwell grinned.

Madison could barely catch her breath. It was only a kiss, for heaven's sake. How could she let herself get carried away? As an actress, she needed to focus. She mentally reprimanded herself.

"You guys look so twitterpated with each other," Patricia said, giggling. "Such a happy couple."

Jared turned away, frowning.

Shelly packed up the camera, and Zachary looked at his watch. "It's been fun, but I have an early day tomorrow. I'm afraid we must be heading out."

Jared stood. "It's time we left as well." He extended his hand to Madison, which she was grateful for as her knees were still wobbly, but when she looked up at him, anger flashed in his eyes.

They said their goodbyes, and she suddenly felt nervous to be alone with him. He was acting like a caged lion, about to spring on her once they were alone. She sucked in a breath and stepped out into the evening, the sun already below the horizon.

5

Jared stalked toward his car, Madison clicking behind him in her heels, trying to keep up.
He was being rude, but he didn't care.

When he was sure no one could see them from
the house he rounded on her. "What did you
think you were doing in there?"

Madison blinked, her eyes wide. "What are
you talking about?"

"Don't you play innocent with me. You were
supposed to look like a crazy chick so my family
would break us up. But instead, you...you do
that! Now they think we're twitterpated."

A laugh erupted from Madison, and she clamped her hand over her mouth.

"What?"

"Sorry, there's just something about an angry CEO shouting the word twitterpated. I've got to add that to my 'things I never thought I'd hear' list."

He couldn't think of a thing to say in response, so he unlocked his car and slid into the driver's seat, huffing in exasperation. She was infuriating. Didn't she realize the position she'd put him in? This was no time to joke.

Madison climbed in the car.

"Don't expect to get paid. After what you pulled, you're lucky I don't file a restraining order."

"Hey, it's not like it was all *my* fault. You were kissing me first."

"I was only trying to appease my aunt."

"Well, you appeased the socks right off me."

Jared stared at her. "What does that even mean?"

"It means, stop kissing people like that unless you want to be kissed back. Now, drive." She motioned toward the driveway.

He narrowed his eyes, annoyed she was telling him what to do, but held his tongue. The engine roared to life and he pulled out onto the street.

Obviously Madison sucked at being an actress. She couldn't even play the simple part of a girlfriend. And her idea of trying to get his family to break them up was insane. He didn't know why he went along with it in the first place. He'd handle this his own way, and hope his aunt wouldn't be too hurt.

"Tomorrow I'll tell them we had a fight on the way home. Next week I can let them know we broke off the engagement."

She folded her arms across her chest. "Sounds like a plan."

When they pulled onto the interstate, he gunned it. The rush of speed made him feel better. He figured it was worth the risk of a ticket if he could make this disaster of an evening end sooner.

Madison didn't say anything. She continued to stare straight ahead out the window. Good. He'd rather sit in silence.

He wove through the traffic, passing cars and trucks. The clock on his dashboard said it was seven fifteen. Less than three hours and he'd be home. Maybe he'd relax in his Jacuzzi before bed. After today, he deserved it.

"You know, this whole thing wouldn't have happened had you simply kept your word and tried to find me a job at your company."

He gaped at her. Was she serious? This was his fault? "Excuse me?"

She flipped her hair over her shoulder. "If you hadn't lied to me about maybe having a position—"

"I didn't lie. I said maybe, and I meant maybe. You're the one who jumped to conclusions about my assistant." He tried not to shout.

"You wanted me to think that. You implied I would get a job if I pretended to be your girlfriend."

"Which you couldn't even pull off," he muttered.

She turned to face him. "Oh, I pulled it off, all right. Your family thinks we're great together. I think Patricia's exact words were, 'Such a happy couple.'"

He scowled at her. "Don't bring my family into this."

She paused, staring at him. "You're a Taurus, aren't you?"

"What?"

A smirk crossed her face. "When's your birthday?"

He rolled his eyes. "Oh. You're one of *those* people." He shot her a sideways glance. "That explains a lot."

"Funny. Let me guess. You were born in May. Maybe around the 5th?"

She was eerily close, but he didn't want to admit it. "I don't believe in that baloney."

"Then just tell me."

"No."

"It's May 5th, isn't it?"

He sighed. "May 7th."

"Ha! I knew it." The smug expression on her face made him grimace.

"Lucky guess."

Her blue eyes bored through him. "You're stubborn, a classic Taurus trait. You're a CEO of a successful company, which shows your determination to go after what you want and not stop until you get it. Your life is boring, but you don't care because you like consistency and stability. You like the finer things in life, and you're not afraid to go after what you want. All these things point to Taurus."

He snorted. "That could describe almost anyone who strives to achieve. Plenty of successful businesspeople weren't born in May. Astrology is a bunch of hokum."

Madison raised her chin defiantly. "You surround yourself with material things to fill the void in your life. You resent your father for his string of wives. You're jealous of your half-brother because he got to grow up with his mother, the one thing you wish you had but didn't as a child. Your father felt guilt over this and compensated by throwing money at you. Your aunt is the only mother figure you've had, so you cling to her approval."

Her words stung, hitting too close to home for him to admit. "You get all that from looking at the stars?"

"No," she said, her tone soft. "I got that from watching you. It's written all over your face. You never got over your parents' divorce."

She'd jumped to a wrong conclusion, and he grabbed onto it with both hands. "My mother *died* when I was a child."

The words hung between them, and her face flushed. "Oh." Her gaze fell to her lap. "I'm sorry."

The silence stretched, until Jared couldn't stand it anymore. "Don't be," he said quietly, feeling bad he'd used that against her. "It was a long time ago."

She fiddled with her hands. "I shouldn't have said those things. Sometimes my mouth gets going and my brain hasn't had time to put up a filter."

"Yeah, I noticed."

"Well, I'm filtering now, let me tell you, because this is not at all what I'd like to say." Her cheeks were pink and she looked like she could bite the head off a boar.

He laughed. He couldn't help it. "You're something else."

"Um, thanks?"

They fell into a silence, which was all right with him. He flipped on the radio to his favorite station, and Mozart filled the car. The rest of the drive home passed quickly.

As they neared her apartment, Madison wiped her cheek, the movement catching Jared's attention. Tears streamed down her face.

Instant guilt flooded him. Was she crying because of him? Sure, he'd been a bit rude to her earlier, but she had no reason to cry over it. "What's the matter?"

"It's just...I...I don't know how I'm going to pay my half of the rent. It's due this week and without a job..." Her voice trailed off and she sniffed.

Oh, sure. This was about the money. He pushed down his annoyance. "Look. I'm not paying you after what you pulled. All you had to do was to pretend to be my girlfriend and I would have given you a thousand dollars. You're the one who screwed up."

She nodded. "I know. I can't do anything right. I'm a failure. I can't even get a job cleaning toilets." She pulled out a tissue and blew her nose, her sobs growing louder.

He searched for something consoling to say. "I'm sure you're not a failure at everything. You just haven't tried everything yet."

She wailed and covered her face with her hands.

This was going downhill and fast. If she didn't stop soon, he'd be forced to pull over, and that was the last thing he wanted. He was only moments away from getting the nutcase out of his car. "Look. You did go all the way to my father's house with me."

She quieted down a bit and lifted her head to peer at him.

"And you did eat my stepmother's cooking." He suppressed a smile, remembering her face when she took that huge spoonful of Irene's special potatoes.

Madison sniffed.

"I guess, for your time, I could pay you half..."

Another wail pierced the air and he succumbed. "All right, all right, I'll pay you the full thousand dollars."

Big eyes stared at him from the passenger seat. "Really? You'd do that for me?"

Anything to get her to shut up. He kept that comment to himself. "Yes. I'll write you a check when we arrive."

His heart tugged as she wiped her nose. She really did look relieved. Maybe it wasn't such a bad thing to pay her. He did promise, after all.

He pulled up to her apartment complex and parked in a stall. After writing out the check, he handed it to her.

She beamed, all trace of sadness gone. "Hey, thanks!" She snatched the check, opened the car door, and then chuckled. "And they said I couldn't act."

⁂

Madison strutted up the sidewalk toward her apartment complex, feeling Jared's stare burning on her back. She suppressed a grin. She'd gotten the best of him in the end. With the check clutched in one hand, and her satchel in the other, she sprinted up the steps. When she got to her door, she stole a glance at Jared. He still sat in his car, glowering.

The jerk. He deserved to know the sting of disappointment. He'd heaped enough of it onto her tonight. But guilt wormed its way into her chest. She had to admit she'd taken her revenge on him too far. It was going to be awkward for him to undo the engagement lie.

She pulled out her keys and let herself in. With a flick, she tossed her bag onto the couch, turned on the light, and shut the door with her foot. The smell of stale cigarette smoke permeated the apartment. She wrinkled her nose. How many times had she begged Carrie to make her boyfriend smoke outside? Yuck. At least they were out tonight, and she didn't have to sit in the living room with them and pretend to care about motorcycles and football.

Her heels were making her feet hurt. She kicked off her shoes as soon as she got into her bedroom, and changed into her oversized t-shirt and sweat pants. Hopefully, her lie wouldn't cause too much conflict in Jared's family. She didn't like the idea of his sick aunt being too upset over it.

The responsible thing would have been to go to bed. However, Madison had never been the responsible type, so she padded into the kitchen and made herself a sandwich. She hadn't eaten much of Irene's dinner, and now her stomach growled.

As she sat at the small dinette munching on her ham and cheese, the image of Jared floated into her mind. Was she crazy to feel a little sad she wouldn't be seeing him again? She giggled thinking of how he'd reacted when she announced their engagement. He sure had the 'deer in the headlights' face down pat.

But he was egotistical and materialistic, not to mention a dirty rotten liar. She'd be insane to want to spend another minute with him. She balled up her napkin and tossed it into the trash on her way out. No, she'd be glad to never see the man again.

She checked her email and her Facebook page. What to put for an update? Staring at the blank box for a couple of minutes didn't give her any ideas. Finally she typed: *Snagged a small acting job. Not a big deal, but it paid well.* There. That was true, and didn't make her look bad.

After brushing her teeth, she crawled into bed. The sheets were freezing, and she pulled the blanket up over her shoulder. Her bedroom was the coldest room in the apartment. She'd even closed the vent, but no matter what, the air conditioning somehow pumped right onto her bed. But if she turned down the thermostat, the rest of the apartment boiled. Maybe she'd get an electric blanket. Seemed silly to use one in the summer, but she couldn't stand the cold any longer.

As she tried to relax, the memory of Jared's kiss floated to the surface. The way he held her close with his hand on the back of her head and his lips exploring hers had sent fire through her veins. Thinking about it warmed her. He could make millions running a kissing booth.

But the kiss didn't mean anything. She knew that. Just a part to play for his family.

She rolled over and pounded her pillow. Best to forget him. No point in spending all night dwelling on the most fabulous kiss she'd ever had. It was over. Much better to go to sleep and forget all about Jared Jameson.

She rolled to her other side, the sweet taste of Jared still on her lips. Dang.

Maybe thinking about the kiss a little more wouldn't hurt anything.

The shrill ring of the phone startled Jared out of a deep sleep. He blinked his eyes, trying to see the clock. Six-thirty. Who would be calling him early on a Saturday? He fumbled on the nightstand, picked up the cordless and growled, "What is it?"

"Jared. It's Patricia."

The emotion in his cousin's voice alarmed him, and he sat up in bed. She wouldn't be calling this early if it wasn't important. "What happened?"

"It's mom. She's in the hospital."

Fully awake now, Jared hopped out of bed. "How bad is it?"

"She collapsed last night...after you left."

"What? Why didn't you call me?" Panic gripped his chest. He snatched a pair of pants from his closet and tugged them on over his boxer shorts.

"They had to run some tests. I didn't want to worry you until we knew."

"Knew what? What do you know? Tell me."

Silence filled the telephone line, and then a small sob. "She's not good, Jared."

His head swam and a lump formed in his throat. "But she was doing better. What are you saying?"

"They aren't sure what happened. They think it's her heart. They have nothing conclusive yet."

Jared swore under his breath.

"She wants you and Madison to come."

"Madison?" His stomach clenched. This could not be good. "Um, she can't come. She's...busy today."

Patricia's voice hitched. "Please, she's insistent. She wants to talk to you and your fiancée."

Dread closed in on him. This was not happening. He had to fix this, and fast. "Actually, we had a fight on the way home."

"Then apologize!" Her voice rose. "This is important, Jared!"

He felt like pond scum. No, lower than pond scum. The slimy pieces of filth that aspired to be pond scum. "Okay, okay. We'll be there."

"Thank you. And please hurry. Mom's kind of agitated."

⁓

The doorbell rang, and then came a knocking, and somewhere in Madison's sleep-deprived mind, she realized she had to get up out of bed and answer it. She doubted Carrie would, after staying out all hours of the night.

Madison pulled on a robe and rushed to the living room. Obviously someone had a problem, with all the pounding going on. She yanked the door open.

The sight of Jared standing there, his dark hair slightly mussed up, his steel-grey eyes boring into her, made her catch her breath.

What's he doing here?

"I'm not giving you the check back." She folded her arms across her chest.

"I'm not here about the money."

His voice sounded funny. Raspy.

She softened her tone. "What do you want, then?"

"Aunt Shelly's in the hospital."

Her hand flew to her mouth. "Oh, no. What happened?"

"She collapsed last night. They're running more tests, but it doesn't look good."

"I'm so sorry." She fiddled with the tie of her robe. "Please tell your family I send my condolences. I hope she gets better soon." She started to close the door, but he pushed it back open.

"You don't understand. She wants to see you."

She'd have been less surprised if he had said he was training monkeys to do the Macarena. "Me! Why me? I barely know her."

He leaned against the door jamb, a scowl forming on his face. "I think it might have something to do with the fact you told her we were engaged."

Guilt flooded her, but she didn't want Jared to see it, so she forced an exaggerated sigh and said, "You make one mistake and no one will let you forget it."

"Funny. Get dressed. We're leaving now."

She made a face. "Fine. It's not like I have a *job* or anything." She held the door open and motioned him inside. "Have a seat. I'll just be a minute."

He seemed relieved she agreed to go with him. Like she was heartless or something and could deny a dying woman's last wish.

She froze.

Oh, heavens, what if his aunt really is dying? What if she makes Madison promise to love, honor and obey Mr. CEO Pants? Can a person go to hell for lying to a dying woman?

Pushing those thoughts away, she threw on some jeans and a blouse, spritzed a little perfume, and walked back into the living room. "Okay, I'm ready."

Jared tried not to stare at Madison, but it wasn't easy. How she could look that good without any makeup was a mystery. Clad in a v-neck blouse and a pair of jeans that showed off her shapely legs, she could easily have come from a fashion magazine photo shoot. He motioned her outside.

When they got to the parking lot, he opened the passenger door for her. She raised her eyebrows at him but didn't say anything as she slid into her seat. Yeah, he had been rude yesterday. He probably deserved her silent treatment.

As he pulled out onto the street, his stomach felt cold and heavy, like he'd swallowed a lead ball. Losing his aunt would be harder on him than he'd like to admit. She'd always been there for him. She'd been the one who consoled him as a child when his mother died, a constant in a world where he had to guard himself from feeling too much for each stepmother who came, showered him with love, then left, never to be heard from again.

Madison played with the small clutch purse on her lap. "You said your aunt was sick. Do you mind if I ask what's wrong?"

His stomach rolled and he gritted his teeth. He didn't want to talk about his aunt. That was none of her business. He liked to keep personal matters to himself. It was better that way. Safer. He hesitated, unsure of what to say.

"I'm sorry. I don't mean to pry. It's just—if we're supposed to be engaged, I probably should know..." Her voice trailed off.

He sighed. She was right. There was no good reason he should keep her in the dark. "She has been fighting cancer in different forms for years. She's been in and out of the hospital. The cancer is gone, thank goodness, but now they think something's wrong with her heart."

Madison nodded, her face grave. "You're obviously close. Tell me about her."

Even though his instinct was to tell her to shut up, he swallowed and resigned to answer her questions. He was forcing her to come with him...to put on this pretense. She had a right to ask about his aunt.

"I was only five when my mother died. Aunt Shelly lived close, so she came over a lot. Helped me through the hard times."

"Must have been difficult for your father, too."

Jared held back a sneer. "Yeah. So tough on him, he went out and found a new wife. Like replacing a light bulb. Here you are, Son. Here's your new mom. Only she left after a year. Aunt Shelly was there to pick up those pieces too."

"She sounds like a lovely woman. Was she ever married?"

"Yes. Patricia's father was an officer in the air force. He died overseas a year before my mother died."

Madison looked down at her lap. "She's been through a lot." A variety of emotions played across her face, none of which he could read.

"She has." A silence settled between them, for which Jared was thankful.

⁂

Madison clutched her purse and followed Jared through the automatic hospital doors. The antiseptic mixed with the distinct smell of old people rushed at her and almost made her gag.

She hated hospitals.

Her nerves jumped as the two of them entered the elevator. She peered up at Jared, who looked like he was playing a game of poker. Stoic. In control. Nicely dressed in a pair of slacks and a polo shirt. He even smelled nice. Was that his aftershave? She leaned a little closer and sniffed. Man, he smelled good. The elevator closed in on her, and she felt light-headed. "Maybe I shouldn't have come."

He raised an eyebrow but didn't say anything.

"See, hospitals and I don't really get along. They give me the heebie jeebies."

He frowned. "You don't have to do anything. You don't even have to say anything. Just walk in with me. Remember, you're the one who—"

"Yeah, yeah, I know." She huffed. "You don't have to keep saying it."

The elevator doors swished open, and she almost ran out. Being penned up in a small place with Jared was playing tricks on her. She almost felt attracted to him.

They entered room 308, and Patricia was immediately at their side. "I'm so glad you're here. Mom's been asking for you." She pushed them toward the bed. Shelly lay there, a white sheet covering her up to her arm pits. She had an IV in one hand, and her face looked even paler than yesterday.

"Jared, Madison...thank you for coming."

Madison glanced around the room. The whole family was there. Mark and Zachary sat in the two chairs. Irene stood looking out the window, her arms crossed. Maxwell stood by his wife, his hand on her shoulder.

"I think you all know I'm dying."

Madison jerked her head toward Shelly and a startled gasp came from Irene. Patricia sobbed into a tissue, and Zachary crossed the room to be by her side.

Maxwell frowned. "Now, Shelly, you shouldn't say such things."

"Hush. Everyone knows it. I'm just brave enough to say it out loud."

Madison stole a glance at Jared. His face was a mask, yet his eyes appeared moist, sad. And when he blinked, a tear escaped and fled down his cheek. She turned away, embarrassed to be privy to his emotion.

Shelly waved her hand. "Now, don't everyone get all upset. I'm ready to go. I'm not afraid of heaven. In fact, I'm looking forward to being with my Henry again."

Several people nodded, and Patricia pulled another tissue from the box on the hospital tray.

"There's only one thing I want done before I go."

Everyone in the room gazed at Shelly, collectively holding their breath.

"I want to see you kids get married." She motioned to the two engaged couples.

ACCIDENTALLY MARRIED

Madison's knees went weak and the room spun. Jared's strong arms wrapped around her and pulled her upright.

Shelly twisted in her bed to look at the calendar on the wall. "The way I see it, this had better get done quickly. How does next week sound?"

Patricia squeezed Shelly's hand. "Of course, Mama. Anything for you." She looked back at Madison and Jared, her eyes pleading.

Madison's throat closed and she couldn't speak. She could barely breathe. She looked at Jared, her eyes wide. He shifted his weight. "Well...um...that's really short notice..."

Patricia glared at him.

"I mean...of course we'll...uh...you know..." His face flushed.

"Two weeks then." Shelly brushed a piece of lint off the bed sheet. "Please? All I want is to see my daughter and my nephew happily married."

Jared swallowed. "Um...well..."

"Okay," Madison said, before she knew what she was doing. "Two weeks. We'll be able to pull a wedding together by then."

Jared looked like he had eaten a live frog.

Irene crossed the room and pulled the two couples into a group hug. "Well, then, we'd better get busy. We've got a double wedding to plan!"

Jared couldn't believe how far things had gone. There was no way he would marry that woman to make his aunt happy. Madison was a fruitcake. A nutcase. She made Paris Hilton look sane. Even if she did look good in those jeans. Then he made the mistake of glancing at her. Yep. She looked good in those jeans. But she was definitely a wack-job.

Irene babbled about flowers and catering, and the urge to end this charade overtook him.

"Excuse me. I need to tell you all something."

Madison knew it was coming. He could tell by the way her eyes got wide and her mouth formed a little 'o'.

"This is not my fiancée."

There. He'd said it. Gotten it out. Cleared things up. He folded his arms across his chest and stared at the confused faces around him. Why didn't he feel better?

Madison threw her arms around his neck. "Of course not officially, sweetie, since we don't have the ring yet. But how important is a ring when we have our love?" She stood on her tip toes and kissed him. A quick peck, but it left him with the warm feeling of her lips against his. Then she whispered, "Don't worry. I have a plan."

He shook his head to clear it. That's all he needed. To follow another one of Madison's deranged plans.

"No. That's not what I meant." He pulled back and Madison dropped her arms. "I mean I'm not getting married—"

"Without a prenup." Madison interrupted, looping her arm through his. "I know it's important to you, darling. And I'm all for it."

Patricia gave him a dirty look, but his father nodded. "Smart boy."

"How can you think of money at a time like this?" Patricia threw him another scowl and clasped Shelly's hand.

"No. That's not it. I just—"

"Excuse me," a nurse with a raspy voice said behind him, "We need to run more tests. I'm afraid everyone will have to come back later."

"Wait. I need—"

Madison tugged him toward the door. "Hush. I said I have a plan."

At a complete loss as to what else to do, he let her usher him down the hallway and around the corner. Her eyes flashed with anger. "Why did you do that? You could have ruined everything. I have an idea that will solve all of this."

"So do I. It's to tell the truth." He stared back at her, arching one eyebrow.

"No, that's no good." She dismissed it with a wave. "Your aunt wants to see us married."

"I have news for you. We're not getting married. We're not dating. I don't even like you." The moment the words left his mouth he regretted them. Hurt showed in her eyes, and she stepped back. He didn't even mean what he'd said. He did like her. The thought startled him. When did he start liking her?

She blinked, and for a second, he thought she would cry. He couldn't stand it. Even her fake crying had made his stomach clench.

Then he spied Mark down the hallway. Without thinking, he pulled her into his arms and kissed her. He told himself it was because Mark was watching, but he knew it was a lame excuse. Madison's lips were intoxicating. Ever since yesterday's five-alarm kiss, he'd been pushing away the urge to do it again. And her little peck in the hospital room had only reminded him how good it felt to have her lips on his.

It didn't take long before Madison responded to his gentle probing. The kiss deepened, and electricity ran through him. She tasted like cherry lip balm, and he found himself wanting to buy a case of it. He'd never tasted anything so good.

When she finally broke the kiss, a questioning look came over her face.

He motioned down the hall with his chin. "Mark was watching us."

"I see." She glanced behind her, to the empty hall.

"He's gone now."

"Yeah. I got that."

Jared realized he was still holding her close. Then he realized he didn't mind it so much. "About the plan..."

She smirked. "I thought you didn't like me."

"That came out wrong."

"How can, 'I don't even like you,' come out wrong?" She wriggled free from his grasp, which left his arms feeling empty. Weird. Being this close to her was playing with his mind.

He sighed. "Just tell me."

She brushed a strand of silky blonde hair from her face. "Okay. I know this guy who's always looking for acting gigs. Why don't we hire him to play our minister? He can 'marry' us," she used air quotes. "Then we can tell your family later it didn't work out." She grinned, like she'd invented Jell-o.

Jared thought about it. It actually wasn't a bad plan. "That might work."

She crossed her arms in triumph. "Thought so."

"Patricia will wonder why I'm not using Pastor Ryan."

She tapped her chin in thought. "Tell her you have your own church in Crimson Ridge. Do you go to church?"

Church. That was a subject for another day. "Not really."

"Then say I have a good friend who is a minister. I have my heart set on using him."

"Using who?" Patricia's voice cut in.

They both jumped and turned. Jared scowled to cover up any hint of guilt.

"Oh. My friend who is a minister." Madison fiddled with her clutch purse. "I was hoping we could use him to marry us."

"Sure." Patricia smiled. "Zachary and I would be fine with using your friend."

"Um...I...uh..." His tongue felt like sandpaper. "I thought you'd like to use Pastor Ryan."

She worried her bottom lip between her teeth. "Well, he has been a close family friend."

Jared clasped his hands. "It's settled then. We'll have two ministers there. Pastor Ryan, and Madison's good friend..."

"Jimmy. I mean, Pastor James." Madison put on a watery smile.

"Two ministers will be great." Patricia beamed and pulled Madison close. "This will be such a special occasion."

"That's one word for it," Jared muttered, relieved they'd gotten themselves out of that mess.

Madison pulled back from Patricia's embrace, guilt tugging at her. She shoved the feeling away. This was no time for that. Guilt wouldn't help her now. She had to muster through this.

Two nurses in blue scrubs rushed past them. A man with an IV drip shuffled his way down the hallway. Irene turned the corner and spotted them. She rushed over. "Here you are. I've been looking for you. We have so much shopping and planning to do. Can you stay in town for a few days?" She glanced between Madison and Jared.

"I don't have to get back. No job." Madison tossed a pointed look at Jared.

The scowl on his face deepened. "I have to get back to the company."

Oh, no. He wasn't going to ditch her and leave her to deal with this by herself. She put her arms around him and snuggled close. Man, he had nice abs. Rock hard. Like his chest. And he smelled good. A light musky cologne, mixed with his laundry detergent. She peered up at him with her best puppy dog face. "Awe, sweetie, can't you take some time off? You work so hard. And it's Saturday."

He put his arms around her, but shook his head. "Sorry, I can't. I usually work weekends."

That didn't work. Jared probably wanted to help plan this wedding about as much as he wanted to shop for tampons. This would take a little more persuasion. She blinked fake tears from her eyes. "But, it's the only wedding we'll ever have."

Patricia joined in. "This is the most important day of your life, Jared." She stood with her hands on her hips.

"We have no clothes here."

Irene put her hand on his arm. "There's a box of your old clothes in the attic. And Madison's about my size. I'm sure she'll fit plenty of things in my closet."

He hesitated, and Madison almost thought he'd relent, but in the end he said, "I'm sorry. There's a lot going on at work."

"It would be nice to have you close in case we get bad news from the tests." Patricia's face was grave.

Jared sighed. "Okay. I'll stay."

Relief flooded through her. She wasn't sure if it was because she didn't have to deal with his family by herself, or because the thought of being around him for the next few days was appealing. Maybe a little of both.

Irene beamed and smoothed her hair. "Great. Let's all meet at the house so we can start planning. I'll prepare the guest room."

Jared stiffened. "No need. We'll stay in a hotel."

"Oh, that's silly. You'll stay in our home. There's plenty of room."

"There's plenty of room in a hotel, too." He clasped Madison's hand and stalked down the hallway, leaving her no choice but to go with him, or be dragged.

When they were out of earshot, she said, "That was rude."

"She has no right to tell me what to do." His footsteps quickened, and she fought to keep up.

"She's your stepmother, and she deserves respect." She tried not to sound out of breath.

They rounded a corner and arrived at the elevators.

"Marriage is nothing more than a piece of paper. And it means even less to someone like my father. She'll be gone next year." He let go of her hand and pressed the call button.

Shock rang through her at his callousness. "She's family, whether you like it or not."

"And soon, she won't be family anymore. That's the way it works around here." The elevator dinged and opened its doors. Jared stepped in, and she got the feeling the discussion was over.

She followed him, pressed the button, and let the doors swish shut. His hands were stuffed in the pockets of his tan slacks, and he avoided her gaze.

Maybe he wanted the discussion to be over, but she wasn't ready for that. "You should apologize."

He glowered. "And you should mind your own business."

Anger arose in her. Who did he think he was? "You don't even know what you have, do you?" She forced the words out, her fingernails digging into her palms.

"What's that supposed to mean?"

"I can't believe you. You treat everyone as if they're beneath you. You're rude, mean, and thoughtless. You step on the people who love you, like they're not even worth your consideration." Heat crept up her neck and her stomach clenched.

Surprise and then another emotion she couldn't read registered on his face, but before he had a chance to say anything, his phone rang. He pulled it out of his pocket, glanced to see who it was, then took the call. "Yes?"

The doors slid open, and the two of them exited to the main lobby. Jared nodded, then said, "All right." He stuffed the phone back in his pocket.

Madison was too mad at him to say anything. She stalked ahead of him toward the sliding doors that led to the parking lot.

"Wait." Jared grabbed her arm, heat searing through her with the contact.

She whirled around to face him, words fighting with her tongue to get out. "You're surrounded by people who love you. People who ignore your mood swings and tolerate your bad manners because they're your family, and that's what a family is supposed to do. Well, I have news for you. Not all *families* are like that." Tears sprung to her eyes, and she turned and fled the building.

Her footfalls echoed in the underground parking lot. Jared's followed close behind. "Madison, stop."

The way he said it made her freeze. Like a caress instead of a command. He came up behind her and put his arms around her. "I'm sorry," he said, his breath brushing her cheek. "You're right. You're right about all of it."

He turned her around to face him. Concern knit his eyebrows together. His steel-grey eyes bored into hers. "But I have a feeling this isn't about me anymore."

Her throat tightened, and she wiped the moisture from her cheeks. She didn't want to talk about it. "You should apologize."

A sadness filled his eyes as he stared at her. He brushed a strand of hair from her face and nodded. "Okay. I will."

8

Jared stared at Madison, pondering what she'd been through to warrant the kind of emotion now splayed across her face. The urge to protect her overcame him. Then he realized he'd been the cause of it. His own thoughtless words.

Remorse plagued him. He was such a fool. When would he learn to keep his mouth shut?

"We'd better go. Patricia wants to make wedding plans." His car beeped when he pressed the unlock button, and he opened the passenger door for her.

The silence blared as he drove. He tried several times to say something, but before the words came out, he changed his mind.

She was right. He treated his family poorly. And they didn't deserve it. She didn't deserve it, either.

They arrived at the house and pulled into the driveway behind Irene's Mercedes. Patricia and Zachary pulled up behind them. No one spoke as they walked up the sidewalk.

Irene opened the door, and Jared stepped forward, his hand on Madison's back. "Irene, I must apologize for the way I acted at the hospital. I'm under a great deal of stress, but I did not mean to take it out on you."

Irene blinked, stammered a bit, and then smiled. "No offense taken. I didn't mean to make you uncomfortable. You can stay wherever you'd like, of course."

"We'd be happy to stay here," Madison said, wrapping her arm through his.

He scowled at her, then smoothed his features into what he hoped was a smile. "Yes."

Irene was obviously pleased. "We'd love to have you."

Patricia elbowed Madison, and they began whispering. Then Madison laughed. He raised his eyebrow at her, but she just shrugged.

They sat in the living room, and Patricia pulled out a notebook and pen. "I thought we'd start by brainstorming. If this is going to happen in two weeks, we'll need to improvise. Get creative. And we'll need to invite people by phone instead of sending out invitations."

Zachary put his arm around Patricia. "We're thinking this will be a small affair. Family and close friends. How does having the wedding here sound, in the backyard?"

Irene nodded. "Perfect. Madison, what about your family? Can they make it on such short notice?"

Jared watched her for a reaction. Madison shifted in her seat. "My, uh, parents died in a car crash. I don't have any other family."

She was lying, he had no doubt in his mind. But, from the way she'd acted earlier, he was guessing there was a good reason she didn't want her family around.

"Oh, I'm so sorry." Irene clutched at the scarf around her neck. "That's terrible."

Patricia clasped Madison's hand. "You poor thing. Surely you must have friends you'd like to invite?"

Madison nodded. "I do. My best friend, Carrie. I'll explain to her what's going on. I'm sure she'll want to be there."

Patricia wrote something on her notepad, then turned to him. "What about you? Who do you want to invite?"

The shocking realization he had no friends crashed through him. The only people he associated with were people who worked for him. They kowtowed to him when he was near, and he was sure they gossiped about him when he was not. Even Darlene hated him. "No," he muttered. "I just want family there."

No one questioned him. Patricia jotted down something else. "I'd like Angela and Casey to be my bridesmaids." She continued to talk about things he couldn't care less about, and he found his mind wandering.

He studied Madison, sitting with her ankles crossed, her soft hair brushing against her shoulders. He found it difficult not to stare at her slender waist and her shapely legs.

"Don't you think so, Jared?"

His head snapped up. What had they said? Should he nod? Or admit to not hearing the question? Patricia stared at him, waiting for a response.

"Yeah. Sounds good."

Patricia smiled. "Great. We'll all write our own vows, then."

He held in a groan. Sure, he had to pick that moment to drift off. How in the world was he going to write fake vows for his big, fat, fake wedding?

He sunk into the couch, and he was sure he heard a giggle coming from Madison. This was going to be a very long two weeks.

⁂

A trio of mannequins dressed in flowing white dresses posed in the window display, surrounded by flowers, tulle, and satin. Madison gulped, while Patricia let out a little squeal of glee. "I can't believe I'm shopping for my wedding dress. It's so exciting, isn't it?" She ushered her into the shop, Irene close on their heels.

The door chimed as they entered. The first thing Madison noticed was the total lack of wedding dresses. Then the plush seating, textured cream wallpaper, and crystal sconces came into view. Her throat went dry. This was no discount store. A saleswoman walked up to them. She peered down her nose at Madison. "Welcome to Claire's. How may I help you today?"

Irene stepped forward. "These two lovely young women would like to try on some wedding dresses."

The woman eyed Irene's designer clothes and plastered on a smile. "Of course. Come, have a seat."

A man in a tux held out a silver tray. "Champagne, ladies?"

They sat sipping their drinks while the sales attendants brought out the most beautiful dresses Madison had ever seen. Patricia's excitement and the royal treatment from the staff calmed her nerves. By the time she picked a few dresses to try on, she was a little excited herself.

Sure, this wasn't a real wedding, but playing the part of a bride would be fun. And Jared would make a great groom. Imagining him in a tux, clean shaven and pulling her close for a dance, weakened her knees.

The first two dresses didn't fit right, but she didn't mind because her favorite was the third. She zipped up the dress and stepped out of the stall. The attendant led her to the mirror room so she could see it from every angle. She stood in the middle of the room and stared at her reflection.

The dress hugged her waist and accentuated her curves. With the right amount of lace and beads, it screamed understated beauty. Her heart fluttered. This was the perfect dress.

Patricia and Irene entered. Patricia covered her mouth with her hand and gasped. "Madison, it's gorgeous!"

Irene beamed. "You look so beautiful. Jared's going to fall over when he sees you."

Madison lifted her arm and flipped over the tag. She choked. Nine thousand dollars? She couldn't afford that! All she had to her name was the check Jared had given her. And $500 was already promised to Carrie for her half of the rent. What was she doing? This was never going to work.

She shook her head. "I'm sorry, this isn't the dress for me."

Irene and Patricia exchanged glances. Then Irene put her hand on her back. "Don't worry about the money. I'd like to pay for it."

Madison stared at Irene. Was she serious? Did she know how much the dress cost?

"I don't have a little girl of my own, and it would mean a lot to me if you let me do this for you." Her eyes darkened with emotion. "I've always wanted a daughter. I'm so lucky you're joining the family."

Blood rushed through her ears, and she felt like she was going to faint. "I don't know what to say." How could she let this woman pay nine thousand dollars for a dress when the whole wedding was a farce? She couldn't do that. She'd feel terrible, knowing the money was going down the drain.

Irene smiled. "You don't have to say anything. I know we've only just met, but I feel like you're already an important part of the family. I see the way Jared looks at you. You make him happy, honey. That's worth so much more than the price of this dress."

"I'm sure we can find a cheaper one."

A frown crossed Irene's face. "But this one...look at it. So beautiful. It looks like it was made for you." Irene put her arm around Madison and gave her a small hug. "I know this rushed wedding can't be what you imagined, but if you can't have the wedding of your dreams, at least you can have the perfect dress."

"But I—"

"Not another word." Irene motioned to the sales woman. "We'll take it."

Madison swallowed. What was she going to do? Maybe she could pay Irene back. After she found a job, of course. She'd save up. Maybe even sell the dress. Yes, she'd find a way to give the money back.

"Thank you," she whispered, emotion making it difficult to speak. Irene was welcoming her into the family, no questions asked, no conditions. Just open arms. The feelings this brought to the surface were strong, and Madison struggled to bury them. This was only an acting job, she reminded herself. This wasn't going to be her real family.

Ten minutes later, they were leaving the dress shop with two wedding dresses ordered. Even though it was getting to be late in the day, the August heat hit them when they stepped outside. Patricia couldn't stop talking about the wedding, and her excited chatter made Madison feel a little better.

As they pulled up to the house, Patricia sucked in a quick breath.

"What?" Irene asked.

Patricia, staring out the passenger window, narrowed her eyes. "That's Veronica's car." A yellow Jaguar convertible sat on the driveway.

Madison wasn't sure if she should know who that was, but decided to take the chance and ask. "Who's Veronica?"

Patricia turned a serious face to her. "Jared hasn't told you?"

"Um, I don't think so."

"That's not good." She chewed on a fingernail, worry lines etched into her forehead. "She's Jared's ex. Come on, we'd better go inside. I'll tell you about her later."

Patricia hopped out of the car and dragged Madison up the walkway and through the house. They found Jared in the living room, sitting on the couch next to a busty brunette wearing cute shorts and a trendy top. Gold bangles jingled on her arms. Her legs were crossed, and her feet were adorned with expensive-looking strappy heels. She was draped over him, and they were looking at what appeared to be a high-school yearbook.

"Remember that? I can't believe your hair." She laughed, a deep throaty sound.

"Hey, it was cool back then." He blushed.

Patricia folded her arms. "Veronica, what brings you here?"

The sound of her voice made them both jump, and Jared's blush deepened. He stood. "Um, Veronica, I'd like you to meet Madison, my fiancée." He rushed over and put his arm around her waist.

Veronica closed the yearbook and stood. "Aw, she's adorable." Her gaze flickered over Patricia. "Good to see you again, Patty."

Patricia stiffened.

Veronica fanned herself. "Jared, I'm a bit hot. Do you mind being a sweetie and getting me a glass of ice water?"

"Sure." Jared left the room.

Veronica meandered over to Patricia, doing a perfect hip-swaying thing. Long red fingernails adorned her hands, which she rested on her hips. "You look good, Patty. Love the haircut. Have you lost weight? You looked a little porky last time I saw you." Her gaze turned to Madison. "And Maddie." She said it like she might address a child. "You're nothing like I thought you'd be. Jared usually goes for the more...sophisticated type."

Patricia's lips tightened into a thin line. "Veronica—"

"Don't worry. I won't get in the way of your wedding plans. I know you have lots to do, with such a rush and all." She eyeballed Madison. "I'm sure there's a good reason for the quickie wedding." She patted Madison's belly, tsked, then crossed the room.

Madison was too stunned to make a sound, her throat closing. Red flamed Patricia's cheeks. "That's not why—"

"You don't have to explain to me, hon."

Jared came back with a glass of ice water and gave it to Veronica. "Here you go."

She took a small sip. "Thank you, darling. You're a life saver." She brazenly kissed him on the cheek. "I must be going now. I'll show myself out." She handed him the glass and sashayed out of the room.

Everyone seemed to be in a trance until the front door slammed.

"Of all the..." Patricia rounded on Jared. "Why did you let her in here?"

"Don't be rude. Just because you don't like her—"

"Don't like her? You should have heard what she said. She's mean, Jared."

He frowned. "She was pleasant. You shouldn't let past quarrels get in the way of how you treat people."

Patricia huffed. "Why was she even here?"

Irene came into the room and set her purse down on a chair. "I take it that was Veronica?"

Jared cleared his throat. "Yes. She stopped by. I guess she saw me out shopping so she knew I was in town."

Patricia rolled her eyes. "Great. I suppose you invited her to the wedding?"

"What was I supposed to do? She's an old friend."

Patricia muttered something under her breath and stomped out of the room.

Jared looked so uncomfortable, Madison decided not to ask any questions. It wasn't like she really was his fiancée, anyway. None of her business. So what if he was into this Vanessa, or whatever her name was. She didn't care.

She peered up at Jared and noted his strong jawline and high cheekbones. He really was a handsome man. And he deserved to find happiness. There was no reason he shouldn't be involved with someone.

Then why did she feel this unbearable jealousy streaming through her?

VICTORINE E. LIESKE

9

Jared stood at the sink, brushing his teeth. The bathroom door was closed, the only thing separating him from Madison. She was in the guest bedroom changing into some of Irene's silky nightwear. He tried not to think about it...just kept scrubbing away. After he had the cleanest teeth in town, he rinsed, spit, and dried off his face.

Was she done changing? He didn't want to barge in on her. He paced the bathroom for a minute, then tentatively knocked on the door.

"Come in," her soft voice called.

He opened the bathroom door. She was in the bed, the covers tucked up to her neck, and laying so close to the edge she had to have one cheek off.

He suppressed a laugh. "Don't worry. I'll sleep on the floor."

Relief flooded her face. "Thanks."

The closet contained a quilt and an extra pillow, which he plopped down in the floor next to the bed. He smoothed out the quilt, then sat down. Not very comfortable, but it was the honorable thing to do.

"Nice pajamas," she said with a giggle in her voice. She was peering down at him over the edge of the bed, her hair falling forward, a cute half-grin on her face.

Jared looked down at the dark blue material. It wouldn't be so bad if it didn't have orange fish with kissy lips all over it. "Yeah. I'm sure Dad gave me these to embarrass me."

"Where does one even purchase fish pajamas?"

He chuckled. "Off the half-price rack, I'm sure."

Her laughter bubbled up, and Jared realized he liked the sound. She didn't politely twitter like many of the girls he'd dated. She wasn't afraid to let it loose. The sound comforted him. Let him know she wasn't trying to hold back. She was being real with him.

He climbed under the blanket and tried to find a comfortable position on the pillow. She propped her head up with her hand, her elbow on the bed. Her gaze flickered over him.

"What?"

"Nothing. Just wondering what you were like as a kid. You're so serious most of the time. Surely you weren't always like that."

"I'm not serious. I'm practical. There's a difference. And yes, I was practical as a kid."

She crinkled her eyebrows. "You didn't do regular kid stuff? Sledding down the monster hill up the street? Playing tag? Dancing in the rain?"

"Sure, I did regular kid stuff. I went sledding and played tag. But I can't say I've ever danced in the rain. That's stupid."

"Oh, you're missing out."

He raised an eyebrow. "Really? Sounds like an idiotic thing to do."

Madison got a faraway look on her face. "There's something freeing about being outside in nature, gentle drops falling from the sky, and letting yourself go. You find the rhythm of heaven."

"Hmm. And here I thought you'd just look like a nutcase to your neighbors."

She laughed, then reached over and turned the switch on the lamp. Darkness filled the room. "Good night."

Soft sounds of her getting situated in the bed came to him. Then silence.

He stared at the ceiling, or at least, what would have been the ceiling if it wasn't pitch black. It was odd, staring into nothing. And odd to know a couple of feet away from him lay Madison.

He felt a weird giddiness thinking about her. What was wrong with him? She was not like any girl he'd ever known. She was kind, yet feisty and witty. She made him want to be around her. When he touched her, there were definite sparks. They had chemistry, no doubt. But something more than the physical attraction was there. He genuinely liked her. That hadn't happened in a long time. It made him want to get to know her better.

"Madison?" he asked, softly.

"What?"

"Tell me about your family."

More rustling came, and then silence. It stretched so long, he thought maybe she'd fallen asleep. Then she spoke. "My mother abandoned me when I was a baby."

When she didn't say anything else, he rolled onto his side. "So, you're adopted?"

A bitter laugh. "No, my mother would never do anything as noble as letting a family adopt me."

More silence. He got the feeling this was hard for her to talk about. But he wanted to know, so he probed again. "What did she do?"

"She pawned me off on Grandma. Just left me there. Said she was going to the store. Didn't come back."

He felt sick. Having dealt with his own abandonment issues, he knew what it could do to a person. "Why did she do that?"

"The party life was too appealing. Didn't like to be tied down. Having a child cramped her style."

"You never saw her again?"

"I wish. At least that would have been tolerable. I'd see her every few months or so. She'd come around when she was out of money. Wasted, and smelling like cigarettes and cheap booze. She'd pretend to be happy to see me. Fawn all over me, hugging me and telling me how proud she was of me. But I knew. She hated me. I could see it in her eyes. I had ruined her life." Emotion tinged her words. "And Grandma could never say no to her. She'd always give her money, and as soon as she got what she wanted, she'd be gone again."

Jared tried to imagine what it would be like to have a parent like that. Of all the stepmothers he'd had, none of them ever showed him anything but kindness. Even when he was terrible to them. "What about your father?"

"I never knew him. I doubt my mother even knows who he is."

"Do you and your grandmother have a good relationship?"

"She died when I was sixteen, but yeah, she made things bearable. She taught me to look on the bright side of life. But she was old, and she had health problems. After she died, I spent a couple of years in the foster care system. My own mother came to court and signed away the rights to me. Like she was selling an old piano she didn't want anymore." Her voice broke, and he knew she was crying.

An incredible urge to put his arms around her and hold her overcame him. But he couldn't. So he lay there instead. "I'm sorry." His words sounded hollow.

He heard movement. Maybe she was wiping away tears. "Don't be. I'm better off without family. My mother's probably sprawled out on someone's kitchen floor right now, too stoned to know what day it is. My father doesn't even know I exist. Another party animal, I'm sure. No, I'm fine the way I am. I worked my way through college. Even got some acting experience. And after I get a job and save up some more money, I'll go back to Hollywood and try again. You'll see me in the movies someday. I'll make something out of my life."

"I know you will." He had no doubt about it. "You're ambitious and tenacious. You'll succeed at whatever you put your mind to."

"Thanks, Jared." Her voice was so low, he almost couldn't hear it. "That means a lot to me."

He rolled over and pulled the blanket up to his chin, ignoring the feelings her words were stirring in him. He barely knew her. There was no reason for him to care for her.

And she was crazy, he reminded himself.

So, why did his lips tingle with the memory of her kiss? Why did his arms long to pull her close? It made no sense. He needed to get his mind off her. This whole fake wedding was playing tricks on him. She wasn't his real fiancée. He simply needed to stay focused.

He closed his eyes, and images of her smiling face came into view. She *was* beautiful, he had to admit. And funny. Smart. He sighed, no longer feeling tired.

"Good night," he whispered.

Her even breathing answered him.

⌒∽⌒

Madison awoke the next morning feeling refreshed. The guest bed was comfortable. And large. King sized, probably. She stretched and peered down at Jared.

He lay cramped up in a little ball, the quilt covering only the top half of him, his legs and bare feet sticking out the bottom. Her heart went out to him. That was very kind of him, to offer to sleep on the floor.

She left him sleeping and crept into the bathroom. A steamy shower sounded perfect. She set the clothes Irene had loaned her on the marble counter and undressed. The hot water cascaded down on her.

She'd had crazy dreams last night of Jared's kisses, his warm touch radiating through her. She had to get a hold of herself. The wild fantasies weren't making it any easier to be near him.

The body soap smelled like almonds and vanilla and was luxurious on her skin. She washed her hair with some fruity shampoo and matching conditioner, which was a treat. Usually, she picked up whatever was on the discount table, and that meant they rarely smelled the same, most of the time not even being the same brand.

She dried off with a soft, fluffy towel, feeling like she was at some fancy resort. Irene's designer clothes fit her nicely. She blow-dried her hair and ran her fingers through it to comb it out. It wasn't ideal, but it was presentable. And no makeup. Again. She shrugged. Oh, well. Jared might as well see her real self. They were getting married in two weeks.

A giggle escaped, and then she silently reprimanded herself. That wasn't something she should be thinking. Getting all googly-eyed over him wasn't going to be of any help to her. In fact, it could get her into a lot of trouble.

She went to the door and knocked, in case Jared was changing in the bedroom. No sound came, so she peeked into the other room. The floor was empty, and the bed made. No sign of Jared.

The house was quiet as she made her way down to the kitchen, but as she neared, she heard voices.

"Your aunt Shelly is thrilled you're moving up the wedding. I wasn't sure you were going to go for it, for a minute there." Irene's airy voice.

"Yeah? Why not?" Jared's deep baritone.

"You were uncomfortable with the idea, I could tell. But if you know she's the right girl, then there's no reason to wait."

Silence.

Madison decided to rescue him from the conversation. She walked around the corner and smiled. "Good morning."

Irene, dressed in a long colorful robe, was taking clean dishes out of the dishwasher and putting them away. "Hello, Madison. How did you sleep?"

"Fine." Her gaze traveled to Jared, still in the ridiculous fish pajamas, sitting on a stool at the island. He was eating a bowl of cereal. His disheveled hair made him look incredibly sexy.

"Would you like me to make you some eggs?" A hopeful smile lit on Irene's face.

Jared coughed, and shook his head slightly. Then pointed to his bowl.

"No, thank you. I'm more of a cereal eater in the morning."

"Sure, dear."

Madison grabbed a bowl and a box of cereal and sat on the stool next to Jared. A lopsided grin filled his face. "One catastrophe avoided," he whispered.

She poked him in the side. "Be nice."

After breakfast, Jared went upstairs to shower. Madison plopped down on the couch and picked up one of Patricia's wedding magazines. When he came down, she almost swallowed her tongue. He was clad in a white t-shirt and a faded pair of blue jeans. The outfit showed off his muscles in a way his stuffy clothes never did.

"Since when do you wear jeans?" Her voice cracked, and heat rushed to her face.

He frowned. "They were in an old box of clothes I had left here."

Irene entered the room. "I knew those would fit you." She brushed a piece of lint from his shoulder then shooed him over to the couch. "Go sit by your bride. Patricia's coming, and we need to go over the menu."

Maxwell came around the corner in his robe and slippers, carrying a newspaper in his hand. He pulled Irene close and kissed her. "Good morning, hon. How're the wedding plans coming along?"

There was something about the way he looked at Irene that caught Madison's attention. His expression was soft. Loving. He really cared for her. She wondered if Jared had ever noticed.

"Things are coming along fine." She fussed with his salt-and-pepper hair a bit. It was a simple gesture, but intimate somehow. Madison felt as though she were witnessing something special. They had a bond.

Maxwell settled in his easy chair, put his legs up, and opened the paper. "You kids go on with your business and ignore me."

The atmosphere in the room was comfortable. Easy. Like sitting in front of a warm fire. Madison couldn't help but envy what they had.

When Patricia arrived, Jared had to scoot a little closer to her on the couch, and he ended up putting his arm around her. She couldn't complain. It felt nice. She snuggled into him, ignoring the nagging feeling she should be careful because her relationship with Jared wasn't real.

10

The sweat forming on Jared's brow had nothing to do with the August heat. He wiped his hands on his jeans and leaned closer to the glass case of engagement rings. Soft classical music played in the background. Plush carpeting and gold accents completed the upscale decor.

"Thinking of popping the question?" The robust saleswoman behind the counter smiled. "You look more nervous than Miley Cyrus in church." She chuckled to herself.

Jared tried not to scowl at the woman. "I just need a simple ring." The prices in the case started at nine hundred dollars and went up from there. He swallowed. This was insane. He couldn't spend that kind of money on a fake ring. Then an idea hit him. "Do you have anything with cubic zirconia?"

A deep frown crossed the woman's face. "We only carry quality diamonds. Besides, your girl deserves something nice, doesn't she?"

He stared at the glass, his vision blurring.

"What's her name?" the sales lady prompted.

"Mmm? Oh, Madison."

She smiled. "A lovely name. How did you two meet?"

The story Madison made up popped into his head, and he swallowed a laugh. She was something else, that's for sure. He'd better watch out if she ever got mad at him again. He'd be in for a ride. Jared cleared his throat. "At the opera."

"Oh, a classy woman. You can't give her anything less than she deserves. You know, you should think of this as an investment. An investment in your future."

Their future. What a joke. They didn't have a future. He nodded absentmindedly.

The sales clerk unlocked the case and brought out a couple of displays for him to look at.

"What do you like about her? What makes Madison special?"

Her image flashed through his mind. "She's like no one else." He thought about their first evening together. How she successfully turned the tables on him. "She's witty. She gets under your skin, you know? And she doesn't let go. But she's sexy and smart. Sometimes I don't know whether to strangle her or kiss her." He realized he was babbling and shut his mouth.

The clerk gave him a knowing smile. "Sounds like love to me."

Jared smirked. Love. Right. If she only knew.

He picked up one of the cheaper ones with a small stone. It didn't look anything like Patricia's rock. He had a sneaking suspicion girls liked to compare that kind of thing. Madison might feel embarrassed if her ring were too small. And of course, if he were really picking out something, he'd spend more. The farce wouldn't look very believable if he bought something too modest. He put it back.

If he was going to do this, he might as well do it right. It wouldn't make sense to purchase a tiny diamond. That would tip-off his family.

What would he purchase, if he were actually getting married? His gaze skimmed the displays.

None of the rings she had brought out of the case were elegant enough.

"You know, you're right. Madison deserves something nice." He moved down several feet, where the rings were more extravagant. "Can I take a look at these?"

The woman clutched her necklace, her smile widening. "Of course, sir."

Jared perused the jewelry until he found one with a swirl of diamonds on each side of the main stone. "Is this silver?"

"Eighteen karat white gold. A beautiful setting. One and a quarter carat diamond. And that's a bridal set, so the wedding band matches the engagement ring." She pulled the ring out and showed him how the two rings separated, then came back together.

He smiled. This was the ring for Madison. It was even the right size. He looked at the tag and coughed when he saw the eight thousand dollar price.

"Um, suppose I purchase a ring and she doesn't say yes?" He tugged on the collar of his t-shirt. "What's your return policy?"

The woman patted her hair. "We have a 60 day total refund return policy. As long as the ring is in the same condition, of course."

Elation lifted him. Perfect. He'd return the ring after the fake wedding. "Then this is the one."

A warm smile lit up her face. "She'll love it." The clerk started taking down his information. When she finished up behind the counter, she placed the fancy ring box into a sack and handed it to him. "Now, don't be nervous. I'm sure she'll say yes."

He left the store feeling almost giddy. Madison was going to flip. He couldn't wait to—

Someone collided with him, hard.

"Oh, I'm so sorry." Veronica turned, her ruby red lips curving into a smile. "Why, Jared, so nice to see you again. Funny how we keep running into each other. What are you doing here?"

"Just some shopping."

"Look at you, in your old clothes. You remind me of the time we went to the lake and rented a motorboat. We had a picnic in the middle of the water. Remember that?" She touched his arm.

He did remember. He'd spent two days planning the picnic. The day had ended with Veronica flirting with his best friend. He took a step back. "Yeah."

The corners of her mouth pulled down. "Whatever happened to us?"

He bristled. "You cheated on me."

She smoothed her hands over his chest. "That was a misunderstanding. I miss you. I miss us." She wrapped her arms around his elbow and kissed his cheek.

He stared down at her. What was she doing? "Veronica, I'm getting married in two weeks."

She batted her eyes at him, and ran her fingers up his arm. "That doesn't mean we can't still be friends."

Her meaning was not lost on him, and his stomach soured. "That's not going to happen." He jerked free from her grasp.

A pout formed on her face. "Honey, don't be like that."

"I'm not your honey. I think it's best if we say goodbye. Don't come to my house. Don't come to the wedding. I don't want to see you again." He unlocked his car with his remote and slid into the driver's seat.

Veronica stood on the sidewalk, a look of shock on her face. Then she turned on her heel and marched down the street.

He didn't care. He pulled out into traffic, officially done with her. How he'd ever been interested in her, he'd never know.

Veronica looked back as she heard Jared's car speed off down the street, her eyes narrowing. If she couldn't get what she wanted as Jared's girl, she'd find another way. Something wasn't right about this wedding, and she was going to find out about it.

But first she needed to return the diamond bracelet Eric had bought her. The man was as dumb as a bag of rocks, but he knew how to give a nice gift. Too bad he broke up with her.

Loser. He'd regret his choice. Even though he was a millionaire, he smelled like fish and laughed through his nose. He'd never find a girl who would date him for his personality.

She waltzed into the jewelry store and handed the bracelet to the clerk. "I need to return this. It doesn't go with my earrings."

Lucky for her, she'd found Jared back in town right after breaking up with Eric. Jared owned his own company down in some two-bit town. He was worth a tidy sum.

"Do you want store credit, or shall I credit the debit card this was purchased with?"

Veronica looked down her nose at the woman behind the counter. Not the owner, obviously, wearing some hideous discount blouse from ShopMart. "I don't want credit. I want cash."

The woman's gaze flickered over to the register. "I'm sorry, ma'am, but it's store policy to put all returns back on the card with which they were paid."

Veronica straightened her spine. She knew how to get things done. "Listen here," she paused and stared at the nametag pinned to her shirt. "Margaret. My boyfriend and I are loyal customers. Do you know who Eric Holloway is? We shop here all the time. I would hate for something like this to ruin your store's perfectly good reputation."

Margaret's face paled. "I, um, will have to call my manager."

"You do that." She crossed her arms and tapped her foot.

The woman went into the back room. Several minutes later, she re-appeared. "I'm sorry, Mr. Holloway prefers the return to go back on his debit card."

Veronica clenched her teeth. "I didn't tell you to call Mr. Holloway. And for your information, he gave me that bracelet. It's mine." She snatched it out of the woman's hand and stalked out of the store.

She'd get a few hundred bucks at the pawn shop.

Then she'd go home and find out all she could about Jared's girl and this rushed wedding.

11

A light evening breeze blew past Madison as she walked on the plush green grass in Maxwell and Irene's beautifully landscaped backyard. A stone wall encompassed a grand area that had flowerbeds, statues, and even a waterfall. A gate led to a stone path with a pond and a gazebo. Orange and yellow flowers dotted everything, and climbing vines created an almost fairytale look.

"We can set up the dance floor here." Patricia motioned to one area. "And have some tables set up over there."

Madison nodded and smiled. This backyard would be perfect. The decorations, her dress, the music, everything would be perfect. Everything except the fact it wasn't real.

Her stomach churned. Could she really go through with this? All his family would be there. And they were so kind to her. She thought about his sick aunt. The look on her face when she found out they would move the wedding forward—pure joy. She couldn't disappoint her.

Calling off the wedding now would only cause them heartache. She and Jared would just need to pretend to get married, go back to Crimson Ridge, and wait until an appropriate time to announce their break up.

It wasn't that bad. Right?

"What do you think?" Patricia stood under a trellis covered in little white flowers. "Should we have the ceremony here?"

"It's lovely."

Patricia beamed. "I think so, too." She approached Madison and linked arms with her. "Everything is going to be so wonderful. A truly picture-perfect wedding." Her gaze fell. "I only wish Mom were feeling better."

"How is she doing?"

Sadness washed over Patricia's face. "She's being released from the hospital tonight. I wish it were good news, but I don't think it is. They've run all kinds of tests, and they all come up negative. They don't know what's wrong. I fear they're giving up."

Madison patted her hand. "They're not giving up. I'm sure they're doing everything they can."

A small nod, almost imperceptible, then Patricia squeezed her hand. "You're right."

"Getting negative results is a good thing. They're ruling things out."

"Yes. I know." Her shoulders slumped. "It's difficult not knowing what's wrong. I feel so helpless." She sniffed, and her chin trembled.

Emotion choked Madison, and she drew Patricia into a hug. "I'm so sorry."

Patricia clung to her, like she was a lifeline. "I am going to miss her so much. She means everything to me."

Madison patted her on the back and consoled her as much as she could. She knew the pain of losing a loved one. She'd never really gotten over losing her grandmother. She'd learned to live with it, and over time, the pain had lessened a bit. But it was always there, just the same.

"Maybe they'll find out what is causing her symptoms, and they'll be able to fix it."

Patricia wiped at her eyes. "That is my sincere hope. Thank you for letting me bawl all over you. You're a true friend."

Guilt bubbled up, and Madison's appetite went scampering over the garden wall. She wasn't a true friend. She was a liar.

Jared opened the patio door and stepped onto the concrete slab. He nodded an acknowledgement. Something about him seemed different. Madison couldn't put her finger on it. Maybe it was the jeans and t-shirt that made him look more like a regular guy and not some stuffy 'suit'.

Patricia glanced at him, then Madison, and smiled. "I'll get out of your hair. You two have some alone time." She wiggled her eyebrows, then gave Madison another quick hug. "Thanks for letting me vent."

After Patricia left, Jared sauntered over to her, his thumbs hooked onto his belt loops. "I think Patricia is expecting us to make out." With a glance back at the house, he pulled her into his arms. "It might be awkward if I don't give you at least one kiss."

Madison's heart pounded against her ribcage. The response to his touch was ridiculous. They weren't a couple. It was silly to get all 'school-girl crush' on him.

He reached up and brushed the hair from her face, his fingers wrapping around her neck, his thumb caressing her cheek. "We should keep up appearances."

"Yes." Why did she sound so breathless?

His grey eyes captivated her. He leaned closer. "We wouldn't want them to find out."

She swallowed. "Right."

His lips met hers and ignited a fire inside. She tried not to kiss him back since this was a fake kiss, but it didn't work. She got wrapped up in the moment. Her body tingled and burned at the same time. His lips moved against hers, sending waves of pleasure through her.

She'd never had anyone kiss her this way before. Her knees grew weak, and she clung to him. When he broke the kiss, she had to catch her breath.

"Well," she finally managed. "I guess we showed them."

His lip twitched. "Yes." He motioned toward the garden path. "Let's take a walk."

He took her hand, which surprised her. What was he doing? First the kiss-to-end-all-kisses, now he was holding her hand? She glanced behind her, thinking maybe Patricia was at the window, but no one was watching. Could he be interested in her?

They walked through the gate and down the path to the gazebo. A waterfall cascaded down large rocks and landed in a pond populated with goldfish. The heat of the day had cooled into a delightful evening. His thumb brushed against the back of her hand and she almost melted. Jared motioned for her to sit on the bench running along the inside of the gazebo.

"This is lovely." Gah, why did she say that? She sounded like a stupid teenager with a crush. Dumb. But she felt like a stupid teenager with a crush, so she supposed she was acting appropriately.

Jared sat next to her, and she noticed a lipstick smudge on his cheek. A burning sensation ignited in her chest, and she turned away. How stupid she was. Here she was thinking he was interested, and he was out kissing Veronica behind her back. She stiffened. "You see Veronica today?"

His eyes widened. "Yeah, how'd you know?"

"Lucky guess."

Acid burned in her stomach. Jared wasn't into her. He was into his rich ex-girlfriend. Of course. That made perfect sense. She and he made no sense at all. She stared at the pond and watched the fish glide under the water.

"I have something for you." He reached into his pocket and pulled out a little box.

A hole opened up in her chest. The fake engagement ring. Great. She took the box and opened it. A gasp escaped. She couldn't help it. The ring was gorgeous. The diamond was larger than any she'd ever seen, and it sparkled in the sunlight.

"Wow. Is this real?"

He chuckled. "Yeah."

"You sure know how to pick a fake engagement ring." She slipped it on her finger. It fit perfectly.

He slid off the bench and got down on one knee. "Will you pretend-marry me, Madison?" The breeze ruffled his hair, and his lips curled up in a half-grin.

Why did he have to be so cute? Why couldn't she pretend-marry someone else? Someone who wouldn't break her heart. She swallowed a lump forming in her throat. "Yes, I will pretend-marry you."

His smile grew, and he stood, pulling her up as well. "Good. I was afraid you'd say no." He drew her close.

She squirmed out of his embrace. How could he go see Veronica, then come home and flirt with her? Anger rose. What a two-timing, manipulative, jerk! She slapped a mosquito off her arm. "Let's go inside. I'm getting eaten alive out here."

12

Madison opened the sliding glass door, Jared close on her heels. Patricia eyed her with one eyebrow raised. "What were you two doing out there?"

Thinking of Jared and Veronica had totally ruined the whole ring-giving thing, but she was an actress, and she needed to play a part. Any girl who had been given a gorgeous ring would be thrilled. She plastered on a big smile, and held up her hand. "I guess it's official now."

Patricia squealed, clasped her hands together, then ran over to Madison and pulled her hand close. "Wow, that's gorgeous! Jared, you really know how to pick out an engagement ring. Look at the setting. Absolutely stunning!"

Patricia continued to gush, while Madison acted like the excited bride she was supposed to be. Jared put his arms around her, tucking her head under his chin, which made her blood boil.

"I know Jared proposed already, but seeing the ring, it's almost like it just happened. Zachary proposed while we were hiking. We had reached a lookout, over the trees and a tiny stream. The sun was setting, and it was breathtaking. We sat on a log, and he brought out the ring. It was amazing." Patricia gazed at Madison. "How did Jared propose?"

The urge to get back at Jared for being with Veronica was too great. "It was really sweet. You see, he knew my favorite ballet was Swan Lake. So he put on a pair of tights and—"

"I did no such thing." Jared released her and took a step back.

Madison touched his arm. "Don't be embarrassed, love. It was adorable." Patricia giggled, and Madison had to swallow a laugh. "He blasted the music on his iPod and played the part of Siegfried, dancing around my apartment, doing jumps and pirouettes, in a leotard and ballet shoes. Then he gave me a single red rose, knelt on the carpet, and recited a poem he wrote."

Patricia gasped, and shoved his shoulder. "Jared! A poem? I didn't know you could write poetry."

Jared's face drained of color, and he appeared to be having trouble breathing.

"Yes. It was really good, too. One of those complicated haiku things."

A look crossed Patricia's face and her eyes widened. "Omygosh! You must write a poem for your vows."

Jared opened his mouth, but nothing came out.

Madison hid a smirk. "What a fantastic idea. Share your great haiku writing talent with everyone at the wedding." She whacked him on the back. "You have such a way with words. You left me speechless."

He shut his mouth, opened it again, and then closed it. Shaking his head, he left the room.

"Awe, he's overwhelmed with emotion. He probably didn't think the poem meant that much to me."

"I can't believe the transformation in him. Before he met you, it's like he was a totally different person."

Yeah, an uptight, inconsiderate, oaf. Madison bit those words back. "He's something else, that's for sure."

"Well, when he looks at you, I can see it in his eyes. He loves you. I wasn't sure that would ever happen. He's had a rough time with women."

Ignoring the comment about Jared loving her, she tilted her head. "How so?"

Patricia bit her lip. "He was so young when his mother died. I'm sure that affected him. And I think he fell hard for Veronica, when he was a teen. She really pulled a number on him. Cheating behind his back. Using him. Manipulating him into buying her whatever she wanted."

Madison's mouth went dry. She knew Veronica was bad, but hadn't thought too much about what she'd done to Jared.

Patricia glanced into the other room and lowered her voice. "She ruined his prom night. She sent Jared off to fetch something from the car, and when he got back inside, she'd disappeared. He found her in the chemistry lab—in a compromising position with his best friend."

Madison sucked in a breath. "How terrible. Why would he even want to be around her now?"

"I don't know. She's horrible. Back in high school, when I tried to warn him about her, she found out, and I became her target."

"What did she do?"

"She poured a milkshake over my head in the lunchroom, then said it was an accident. She spread lies about me. Made my life a living hell. But somehow she explained it all away. Made it seem like I was the crazy one. Jared never saw her for what she really was."

Madison thought about what it must have been like for Patricia. She knew what being bullied felt like. She'd had enough of that at school when all her grandmother could afford was clothes from the second-hand store. "I can't believe Jared is still into her."

Patricia stiffened. "You think he's still in love with Veronica?"

Madison realized her mistake, and tried to backpedal. "Oh, well, you know. He still talks to her and stuff. That's all I meant."

"You watch out for her. If she had her way, I'm sure you'd be out the door and she'd be back to sucking the life out of him. You gotta let her know you're not going anywhere. You and Jared are in love, and she can't worm her way in between."

Madison frowned. Veronica was already working her way in. Unfortunately, Madison had no claim on Jared. He was a free man, in reality. He could go back to Veronica if he wanted. Although the thought of Jared being taken advantage of by that conniving she-devil made her skin crawl. Maybe she could find a way to make Jared see what Veronica was truly like.

"I'll keep an eye on things." Madison shifted her weight.

"Yes. And I'll try to talk some reason into him. Why he invited her to the wedding is beyond me." She glanced out at the dark backyard. "I'd better go. Zachary is waiting for me." She patted Madison's arm before leaving the room.

It was late, and the long day had worn on her. She would appreciate slipping under the covers. Madison sprinted up the stairs. When she entered the guest bedroom, Jared rounded on her. "What was that all about?"

"What?"

He glowered at her and folded his arms across his chest. "Tights? Really? What did I do to deserve that?"

She dug her fingernails into her palm to keep from laughing. "Oh, that." She bit her lip. If Veronica was really as bad as Patricia made out, maybe it wasn't his fault. Maybe she was coming on to him. She suddenly felt bad for him. "Sorry."

"You're sorry?" Frustration rolled off him, and he began to pace the room like a caged panther. "Now I have to write a poem for my wedding vows. Oh, but not just any poem. A friggen haiku, for heaven's sake."

A giggle escaped and she clamped her hand over her mouth.

"Yeah, real funny. You know, I can't figure you out. Just when I think we're getting along, you pull something like this."

"I'm sorry. I got a little upset at you."

"Saying I sing you to sleep would be a little upset. Putting me in tights and writing poetry? That's serious." Jared's hooded gaze traveled over her. "Spill it. What did I do?"

"I, uh...guess I felt bad you were sneaking off to see Veronica." She paused to gauge his expression. Surprise flitted across his face. She rushed on. "I mean, I know we're not really getting married. But we should keep up appearances, right? What if someone saw you and her together?"

Jared stepped forward and wrapped his large hand around her arm. "I'm going to say this once, and only once."

The way he was so serious took her aback, and she simply nodded.

"There is nothing between Veronica and me. Nothing."

His intense gaze and close proximity played havoc with her heart, causing it to beat erratically. "But I thought—"

He put his finger on her lips. "You don't have to worry about Veronica. I know how she is. And it's not her I'm fake-marrying." He brushed her hair behind her shoulder, and tilted her chin up with his knuckle. "It's you."

Before she had the chance to think, his lips were on hers. It was a hungry kiss full of passion and urgency. Her hands entwined in his hair, and he pulled her close. His lips roamed to her jaw, then her earlobe. A fire burned in her, and she closed her eyes. The world began to spin.

His kiss came back to her lips, more demanding and more passionate. Her concerns about Veronica melted away, and all that was left was Jared. His kiss created a whirlwind of emotion in her, and she couldn't get enough of him.

He pressed closer until she had to take several steps back. Her legs hit the bed. He began to lower her down, and the realization of what he was doing crashed through her. She jerked away from him. "Wait."

"What?" Desire filled his eyes.

"What are you doing?"

His mouth quirked in a half-smile. "I'm kissing my soon-to-be wife."

"Fake-wife. This isn't real, Jared."

His thumb caressed her back. "What I'm feeling right now is real."

She was backed up against the bed and couldn't step away from him, so she pushed against his chest, which was kind of like pushing against the Great Wall of China. He didn't budge. "What you're feeling right now won't last. You're not in love with me. If we do this, where will we be tomorrow?"

A wicked look crossed his face. "Tomorrow we'll wake up right here. In this bed."

She hopped up on the mattress and backed away from him. "I have news for you. I will be in the bed. You will be on the floor." She jumped down then fled to the bathroom, her heart pounding.

It took a few minutes for her hands to stop shaking and her breathing to become normal. She leaned over the sink and splashed water on her face. Sleeping with him was out of the question. She was already becoming too emotionally attached for her own good. If she allowed it, she'd fall in love, and he'd walk away and never look back.

Becoming involved would only lead to her heart breaking. The bitter pain of feeling used and thrown away. She couldn't allow it. She'd had enough of that her whole life.

Her mother was quite practiced in sucking her dry then tossing her out. The only thing her mother knew how to do was take. Take interest, take advantage, then take the nearest exit. Too bad she never learned to take responsibility.

Saying no to Jared was the right thing to do. Not that she wanted to. His touch sent her over the edge. She could have easily given herself fully to him. But that was the problem. She'd be giving all of herself, and he wouldn't.

Her feelings for him were growing. How had she let that happen? And how was she going to pretend this much longer, without getting hurt?

She pulled on Irene's pajamas and leaned against the door, unsure of what she should do next.

⌒

A string of curses ran through Jared's mind as he paced the floor. What had he done? Of all the stupid things, he had to go and ruin everything. Now Madison was locked in the bathroom and probably afraid to come out.

No wonder. He was such a selfish jerk.

Obviously he didn't love her. He'd only known her for three days. You can't fall in love with someone that fast. Right?

But her kiss had awakened feelings in him he thought were long dead. Passion and longing that he was having trouble fighting. He hoped she'd felt it too.

She hadn't. Or maybe she had, but was being more sensible.

Madison was right. They couldn't take their relationship to the next level. They didn't love each other. And sleeping together would only complicate things.

He sighed and pulled out the pillow and blanket from the closet. He tossed them on the floor, changed, then turned out the light. The floor seemed harder than the previous night, and he struggled to find a comfortable position.

The seconds ticked by, with Madison still in the bathroom. No reason to pressure her. He'd wait.

Finally, the door opened and she snuck over to the bed. She might have thought he was asleep. There were some rustling noises of her settling under the covers, and then silence.

He felt like such a cad for the way he'd treated her, but unsure of how to broach the subject. "I'm sorry." It seemed lame, but it was all that came out.

"I'm sorry, too." Her voice was quiet.

Surprise hit him. "What are *you* sorry for?"

"For getting us into this mess. It's my fault. I shouldn't have."

Her voice held so much remorse, he felt it, like a wet blanket pressing down on him. And yet, it wasn't all her fault. He had brought some of it on himself. And she…he hated to admit it, but she had brought a life back into his existence that he had not had in a long time. Because of her, he got out of bed a little earlier. His steps fell a little lighter. His heart beat a little faster.

She made the world a better place. And he couldn't stand to see her down.

"But not sorry for the haiku crap?"

She laughed, and the mood lightened.

"You know, you're forcing me to become a plagiarist. I don't know the difference between a haiku and a cumquat. I'm going to have to steal one from some poor schmuck on the Internet. I just hope the police don't find out and arrest me at my wedding."

Her laughter came louder now, and he reveled in the sound. "I suppose you could write a limerick instead," she said between giggles.

The thought of him reciting a limerick at his wedding made him snort, which sent them both into hysterics. His sides began to hurt, and by the time they'd settled down, he had to wipe moisture from his eyes. "I don't think I've laughed that hard, ever."

"I didn't think it was possible. You're always so serious."

He thought about the time he and Patricia put on clown noses and rode the city bus the entire route. He'd been fourteen, she twelve, and both had been bored out of their minds. "Not always."

A silence settled in. After a few minutes, he heard, "Good night, Jared."

He smiled into the darkness. "Good night, Madison."

13

Veronica tapped her long nails on the marble countertop, waiting for Rosa to finish making her latte. She tugged on her silk robe, becoming impatient. It was Monday morning, and she wanted to start digging around. Jared was hiding something; she knew it.

"Rosa, if you'd wake up earlier, you'd have time to get my morning coffee ready." She hoped her frown and disapproving tone were enough to whip Rosa into shape. She didn't want to fire her. It was always such a pain to interview.

The little round woman mumbled something in Spanish and scooped the foam off the top of the drink.

"And this is an English-only house. You know I don't like it when you speak that foreign tongue. Then I can't understand you."

Rosa handed her the mug and smoothed her apron. "I'm sorry, Señorita, but you did hire me to keep house. Making your lattes was not in my job description."

"No back talk." Veronica clapped her hands twice. "Now go clean the bathroom. I've got work to do."

Rosa bustled out of the room muttering more Spanish. Veronica rolled her eyes and ignored it.

She took a sip of her drink and let the heat slide down her throat. Much better. She sat down on the barstool in front of her laptop and typed in Jameson Technologies. Then she picked up the phone and dialed the number.

"Yes, Mr. Jameson's office, please."

Soft elevator music played on the line, and then a click. "This is Mr. Jameson's office. How may I help you?" By the gravely sound of the voice, Veronica supposed she was talking to a heavy smoker.

"I am a personal friend of Jared's, and I have an embarrassing problem I'm hoping you can help me with. You see, I'm filling out the card for the wedding gift I'm giving to him and his happy bride, Madison. However, I can't remember her last name. I was hoping you could tell me."

There was a long pause on the other end of the line. "Um, I think you have the wrong number. Mr. Jameson isn't engaged. In fact, I don't think he's even dating."

Veronica sat up straighter. "No, I'm sure I have the right number. I've known Jared Jameson for years. And I know for a fact he's getting married. He told me himself."

"Huh. Well, I haven't heard a thing about a wedding. But you know, he did call in this morning acting strange. Said he's taking a few days off. And he left early on Friday. In fact, he left with a woman, now that you mention it."

"A perky blonde with no fashion sense?"

"I think she was blonde. I can't really remember."

Frustration rose in Veronica. "And I suppose you can't tell me her name?"

"No. Mr. Jameson just said he was waiting for a woman, and to let her in when she arrived because she was late and he had better things to do than wait for her in the lobby. He never told me her name, and I've never seen her around before."

"Well, you've been no help at all." Veronica hung up the phone and tossed it on the counter.

How was she going to find Madison's last name? All she knew about her was she was an aspiring actress from Crimson Ridge. She tried to think of what else Jared said, but she hadn't been paying attention at the time.

Where would actresses hang out in Crimson Ridge? Did they have a community theatre? She pulled up a Google screen and did a search. Bingo. Crimson Ridge Community Playhouse. Live performances each weekend.

She dialed the number. A man answered on the third ring.

"Hi. I need to get a hold of this actress named Madison, however I've misplaced her phone number, and I was wondering if she's involved in the playhouse at all? Do you know a Madison?"

"Madison Nichols?"

A wave of excitement shot through Veronica. "The woman I met had shoulder-length blonde hair."

"Yep, that's her. A real sweetie. I don't have her phone number, but she lives in the old apartment complex up on Juniper Street. Roommates with some hot chick named Carrie."

"Thanks. You've been very helpful."

With a last name, finding Madison's phone number online was a snap. A girl answered on the first ring.

"Hi, you don't know me, but I'm a good friend of Jared's."

The girl hesitated. "Oh, hi."

Veronica smiled and tried to sound sweet. "I was just calling because I'm a little worried about this wedding."

Another pause. "Yeah?"

"Jared and I have been friends for a long time. In fact, we used to date. It got really serious. He actually proposed to me, but I made a mistake and told him no." She produced fake tears and tried to sound choked up. "And now I find out he's getting married to Madison. I feel like he's rushing into it."

The girl on the other end cleared her throat. "Well, you should probably talk to him."

"Oh, I've tried. He's not taking my calls. I'm afraid I've hurt him, and now he's rushing into something he'll regret later. I do still love him.

And that's why I'm calling. How long have they been dating? He and Madison?"

The girl on the other end of the line sighed. "I don't know. A little while?"

"Does he..." Veronica made her voice crack. "Does he love her? Will she make him happy?"

"You know, I shouldn't tell you this, but you sound like you really care for Jared. This thing with Madison, it's not real."

Veronica's heart sped up. "What do you mean?"

"I guess his relative is real sick, and they're pretending to get married because her dying wish is to see Jared's wedding...or something like that. They're not even dating. Jared hired her to play the part of his girlfriend, and somehow they got roped into this whole wedding thing."

Excitement bubbled through her. This was even better than she thought. "But, how can you fake a wedding?"

"They're hiring an actor friend to marry them. It's all just a show."

Jackpot! Her instincts had told her something wasn't right, and boy had they paid off. She exhaled. "Thank God. I was so worried about Jared."

"You won't tell anyone, right?"

Veronica smiled. "Cross my heart."

Jared awoke and took in the made bed and empty bathroom. Madison...the early riser. He hoped things wouldn't be weird between them now. He'd made a mistake. Let his attraction take control. Hopefully, she wouldn't let that come between them.

He undressed and got in the shower, letting the warm water ease his tension. He would need to be more careful in the future. Not let her get too close, especially if they were alone. Madison had no idea how she affected him.

He toweled dry, threw on a robe, and lathered his face to shave. Did she feel anything when they kissed? Or was it all one-sided? The razor nicked his skin as he shaved. He hadn't been paying attention. Swearing under his breath, he pressed a tissue to his face to stop the bleeding.

After he got dressed, he headed down the stairs to eat breakfast. He heard talking in the living room, so he took a detour.

Maxwell sat on the couch next to Madison, a leather photo album on her lap. "And here's the seventh grade spelling bee. Jared got second place."

Jared leaned over to see what his father was pointing at. "You saved that newspaper clipping?"

Maxwell raised his eyebrows. "I saved all the articles about you."

"And you put them in an album? Since when do you scrapbook?"

"Jeannine started the scrapbook. I just kept up with it after the divorce."

Jeannine. Step-mom number three. Mark's mother. She was definitely one of the more sentimental ones. "Huh." That was all he could think to say.

Madison raised her gaze to his face. "You never told me you could bowl. You were on a team. That's so cool."

"The Lucky Five." He chuckled. "We were freshmen, with nothing to do. We thought forming a team and joining the bowling league would impress the girls. It didn't." He slid onto the couch next to her.

"You had cool jackets."

"I think you're obligated to say that, you being my fiancée and all."

Maxwell laughed, the sound coming up from deep in his chest. "I'd love to sit here and reminisce all day, but I'd better get something done."

"What do you have to do? You're retired." Jared looked over at his father, a teasing smile tugging on his mouth.

"Yeah, but now that I'm no longer working, everyone wants free legal advice. I think I'm busier now than I was before I retired." He stood and walked toward his den. "I'd better go check my email."

Madison turned the page and there was a photo of him and Veronica on prom night. He cringed, and turned the page again.

There were his high-school graduation photos. "Look at you. Such long hair!" Madison giggled.

"What is it with the hair?" he mumbled.

"Nothing. You were cute."

He raised an eyebrow at her. "Were?"

She patted his cheek, her touch sending sparks over his skin. "Still are, sweetie."

Irene cleared her throat, which made them both jump. "You two are adorable." She took a rag and a bottle of window cleaner over to the sliding glass door and began to scrub.

For some unknown reason, Jared began to feel self-conscious with Irene in the room. When the doorbell rang, he stood. "I'll get it."

He opened the door and took a step back. "Veronica?"

"Hello, sweetie. I don't mean to be a bother, but can I come in?" She had one hand on the door jam, one hand on her hip, and she was smacking on a piece of gum. Her hair was pinned up in the back in some kind of fancy do, and she smelled of expensive perfume.

He frowned. "What do you want?"

She tapped her long nails on the wood. "You're not going to invite me in?"

"I already told you. There's nothing we have to say to each other."

She slid her gaze over him. "All right. If you want to do this here, fine. I know about you and Madison. I know she's not really your fiancée."

The blood rushed from his face. He stepped outside and closed the door behind him. He grabbed her arm and tugged her around the side of the house. The morning sun created a shadowed area, where no one would see them. "What's this about?"

She jerked her arm out of his grasp. "I know Madison's an actress you hired, that you're not really engaged, and you've hired an actor to pretend to marry you. And I can prove it." Her eyes narrowed into slits. "And I'm prepared to tell your family everything."

He stepped back, his head reeling and his stomach clenching. "Why would you do that?"

She smirked and folded her arms across her chest. "So it's true."

Jared stared at her. He didn't want to admit such a thing to her. But she obviously found out somehow. No use in denying it.

The words wouldn't come out. Instead, he ran his fingers through his hair. "Listen, Aunt Shelly is very ill. She may be dying. She wanted to see us happily married."

Veronica's lips curled down. "Awe, so sorry to hear that, darling." She reached out to touch his chest, but he took another step back. Her frown turned into a sneer. "No reason to be rude."

"Stop it. I told you there's nothing between us, Veronica."

She looked at him, like she might look at a bug on her fine table cloth. "I see how it's going to be, then. We can do this in a more business-like fashion. I want fifty thousand dollars for my silence."

Jared laughed, taking a page in Madison's book, and letting it loose. "You want what?" He laughed again. "If you think I'm going to do anything of the sort, you're crazy."

For the first time, Veronica appeared to have no words. She blinked and her mouth hung open a bit, like someone had slapped her in the face.

Jared continued to chuckle.

She scowled. "Fine. Have it your way." She pulled out her phone. "Is your aunt at home, or is she in the hospital?"

His heart skipped a beat. "You wouldn't."

She raised an eyebrow and swiped her finger over her phone. "Wouldn't I?"

He snatched her phone. "Don't even joke about that. She's very sick."

"Then pay me the fifty thousand dollars."

His stomach soured and bile rose in his throat. "You disgust me."

A smug smile appeared on her face. "I don't care. You never were worth the time I spent on you." She plucked her phone from his hand and turned on her heel. She picked her way through the grass toward her car, wobbling on her heels as they pierced into the earth. "I'll expect your first payment check tomorrow. Ten thousand.

Get it together by then, or I'm calling your dear aunt Shelly."

Maxwell scrubbed his hand over his face and peered out the window. He'd only opened it to let in the morning breeze. He never meant to eavesdrop.

14

Maxwell slid the window shut. Jared and Madison...not really a couple? The news shocked him. He knew Jared had commitment issues, but never thought he'd do something like this.

He sat back down at his computer, not seeing the screen. Why would Jared hire a girlfriend? And why would he pretend they were engaged? It didn't make a lot of sense. Sure, he'd put some pressure on Jared to find someone. Maybe too much pressure, he admitted reluctantly. But he only wanted him to be happy.

He thought back to when Jared first told him he was seriously dating. It was Easter. They were gathered around the table, trying to choke down Irene's dry ham and cold scalloped potatoes. Maxwell asked if Jared had anyone in his life. Before he could answer, Shelly said something about how worried she was about him being alone. Then Mark made a comment about his sexual orientation. That's when he announced he had met someone.

At the time, he'd wondered if it were true. Seemed like something Jared said to get everyone off his case. Jared was evasive when questioned. His instinct must have been right. And as they talked on the phone, he'd ask if they were still dating. He had been pushy, looking back.

And he'd practically hounded him to bring her to his birthday celebration. No wonder he felt backed into a corner. But hire an actress? What was Jared thinking?

And there was no need to tell everyone he was engaged. What purpose did that serve? Wait. It hadn't been Jared who made the announcement. It had been Madison.

Maxwell chuckled, now remembering the look on Jared's face when Madison informed them of their engagement. He wasn't sure exactly what happened, but he was positive she'd surprised him.

And then Shelly collapsed, ended up in the hospital, and asked them to move up the wedding. Caught between the lie and disappointing his aunt, Jared must have decided to go through with the charade.

His leather chair squeaked as he shifted. Something was still bugging him. Maxwell saw how Jared looked at Madison. The sidelong glances. The way his lip twitched when he was trying not to smile. Jared was developing feelings for her. Real ones.

And Madison—if she wasn't in love with Jared, he'd eat Irene's greasy, two-pound cheese soufflé. The way she gazed at him said it all.

Maxwell touched the tips of his fingers together. They were falling in love. They just needed more time together to figure it out.

And Veronica could be dealt with pretty easily. Blackmail only works if the secret is still a secret. He picked up the phone and pressed the speed dial.

"Shelly? It's Max. You're never going to believe this."

Jared stomped up the stairs and slammed the bedroom door. How dare she? Fifty thousand dollars! What, did she think he kept that kind of money sitting in the bank? Of all the stupid...

Madison opened the door. "What's going on? It sounded like an elephant stampeded through the house."

Jared let out an exasperated breath. He didn't want to tell her. Didn't want to admit he was being manipulated by the pathetic waste of human flesh named Veronica. It was prideful, but he didn't care. He was embarrassed to not have seen through her façade before now. "It's nothing."

"Really?" Madison arched one eyebrow, one hand on her hip. "Nothing? You look like you're about to breathe fire."

Jared plopped down on the edge of the bed. "It's something I have to deal with, that's all."

Madison's gaze swept over him. Then she sat next to him and rested her hand on his leg. "Honey, if we're going to make this marriage work, we're going to have to learn to open up to each other." She batted her eyes at him, and her mouth quirked.

He was too mad to laugh, but his mood lightened considerably. "Funny."

"Just tell me what's got you all worked up. It can't be that bad, can it?"

He stared at her big blue eyes, trusting, and suddenly he wanted to tell her. He didn't know why. He was used to keeping things to himself. But for some reason, the urge overcame him. "Veronica found out about us. She's threatening to tell if I don't give her fifty thousand dollars."

Madison sucked in a breath. "What? I can't believe it. Why would she do that?"

"Because she's psychotic." Which was a good description of Veronica. She'd been poison from the start. He should have seen it.

Madison bit her lip. "Maybe we can beat her at her own game."

He could see the wheels turning in her head, and apprehension filled him. Her insane ideas never worked the way they were supposed to. "You have that look on your face."

"Hush. I'm thinking."

"That's what I'm afraid of."

She tossed him a stony expression. "I'm helping. What exactly did she say?"

He sighed. "She knows I hired you to pretend to be my fiancée. If I don't pay, she's going to tell Shelly."

"We could call her bluff. She wants money. I'm not convinced she would talk to Shelly if she didn't get her way. What if you simply didn't pay?"

"That's your big plan? Not pay?"

"Well," she said slowly. "She might not tell her. But in case she does say something, we just need to tell Shelly you did hire me to pretend to be your girlfriend...maybe to ward off some chick at the office. And that's really how we met four months ago. But we fell in love. The engagement is real. Veronica overheard stuff and got it a little wrong."

Jared quirked his head. It wasn't a bad idea. Actually, it was a pretty good idea. It might work. "So, we confess to lying about how we met."

A smile spread across her face. "Yes. We were embarrassed about the whole hiring thing. So we made up the opera story."

He rolled his eyes. "Yeah, because meeting in the women's bathroom was much less embarrassing."

Madison let out a belly laugh, then clamped her lips together and cleared her throat. "Sorry about that."

She was sure cute when she was trying to put on a straight face. "No you're not."

"You're right." A giggle escaped. "Every time I imagine you stumbling around the ladies room, literally bumping into women, it's hard not to laugh."

He hid a smile. "You're thinking of it right now, aren't you?"

She whacked his arm. "Stop trying to make me laugh."

"All right. How about we confess that I didn't hire you to work at Jameson Technologies, but hired you to be my girlfriend instead. Then we don't have to change much of our story."

"Perfect." Her smile made her glow. Something about her made him want to be closer to her. Learn all he could about her. She intrigued him like no other woman ever had.

He brushed her cheek with the back of his knuckles and reveled in the feel of her velvety skin. The urge to kiss her flooded him, but he pushed it away. The last thing he wanted to do was take advantage of her. She deserved better.

He pulled his hand away, and she stared down at her lap, her eyelashes brushing her cheeks. "We'd better gather our things. I'd like to visit Shelly, then I need to get to the office before they let Darlene take over."

She nodded, but he thought he saw disappointment flit across her face before it vanished.

⚯

Madison put on the clothes she had worn out to Highland Falls. Irene had washed them for her. There wasn't much to pack. A toothbrush and hairbrush she'd bought at the department store. A pack of Tic Tacs from the gas station. She stuffed them in her purse.

Why did it feel like she was preparing for a funeral? It was ridiculous. No need to be sad about leaving. It wasn't like they were really engaged. But even as the thought surfaced, she knew the truth. She had deeper feelings for Jared than she wanted to admit.

The way his lip twitched when he was trying not to smile. The sadness in his eyes when he talked about his mother. The way she felt when she was with him. All reasons to get through this fake-wedding, then get as far away from him as possible. He didn't love her. And the more she allowed herself to fantasize, the more it would hurt when they parted.

Jared stuck his head in the room. "We've got a problem."

Her head jerked up. "What?" His face looked so serious, her heart raced to her toes. "Is it Shelly? Is she okay?"

He put his hand up. "No, nothing like that. My father's giving us an engagement gift."

A gift? How was that a problem? "What's he giving us?"

"Two tickets to the Henry Doorly Zoo."

What an odd engagement present. She tried to plaster on a smile. "Okay. Tell him thanks."

Jared rubbed the back of his neck. "They're only good today. I guess he got some kind of deal on them. They include the IMAX theater, and he's insisting we go...have some alone time."

Several emotions raced through her, grappling with each other to see who would come out on top. Happiness, at the thought of being able to delay their separation by a few hours. Dread, knowing she was walking on the edge of a cliff, about to fall off. And amusement, at the thought of Jared at the zoo. The happiness and amusement won out, and she smiled. "Sounds like fun."

"Really? Because I could tell him I must get back to work..."

Her chest tightened. "No. Don't do that. My horoscope today says I should not make waves. I think we should thank him and go."

"When did you check your horoscope?"

"When you were in the shower. I borrowed your phone."

A wary look crossed his face. "How often have you done that?"

She plastered on a sheepish look. "Every day. I...uh, installed an app."

"Is that why I've been getting texts from that psychic Madame Geary?"

"Oh, she's good. You should call her."

He pinched his lips and closed his eyes. When he opened them, she could tell he was trying not to yell. "Just check your horoscope in the paper, okay?"

"Sure. No problem."

He fingered the door handle. "There's one other thing. The zoo is an hour away, in the opposite direction. If we stop by Aunt Shelly's house, then head to the zoo, we won't have enough time to drive home. We'll have to come back here and spend the night tonight."

She tried to keep her heart from hammering in her chest. "That's fine, we can spend another night here."

"All right. I'll go tell my father."

Madison changed into one of Irene's cute sundresses, perfect for a day outside. She slipped her feet into a pair of beaded sandals, glad she and Irene were the same size. Then she stuffed her clothes in the dresser drawer and tossed her toothbrush and hairbrush on the bathroom counter. On her way to the stairs, she stopped at the first door on the left. It was the only room where the door had remained closed, and she had no idea what was in there. Maybe it was a closet. She tried the handle, but it was locked. Who would lock a closet? She shrugged and continued down.

Maxwell and Irene practically shoved them out the door, telling them to have fun and to come back hungry because they were planning a special dinner. Jared raised his eyebrows but didn't say anything.

Shelly's house wasn't far, although the neighborhood was very different. Smaller homes and much closer together, but still an affluent part of town. They rang the doorbell and Patricia answered.

"I'm so glad you're here. Mom's been grouchy and taking it out on me."

A voice from the other room called out, "I can hear you, ya know."

Patricia rolled her eyes. "See what I mean?" She waved them inside, shut the door, then lowered her voice. "She's been having trouble breathing today."

Jared's face paled, and Madison touched his arm, hoping the gesture would let him know she was there for him.

Patricia called out, "Mom, Jared and Madison are here to see you."

"I know. It's not my ears that are having trouble."

"Geesh. Go on in." Patricia turned on her heel and disappeared.

They entered a hallway, then a light-blue bedroom with white accents. The furniture was all antique. Beautiful pieces. Shelly lay in an old-style poster bed, pillows propping up her head and upper body.

"Hey, Shelly. How are you doing?" Jared bent down and gave her a hug. Shelly motioned for Madison to come closer.

"Terrible, sweetie, but don't let me get you down. I heard you're going to spend the day doing something fun."

Jared raised an eyebrow. "Word sure gets around fast, huh?"

Shelly laughed, and a wheezing sound filled the room. "Was just talking to your father. I do have some good news."

"Yes?"

"The doctors say my heart is strong. Whatever is wrong, it's not heart disease."

Jared smiled, but it didn't reach his eyes. "I'm glad. That is good news."

They chatted for a few minutes, and then Shelly seemed to grow tired. "Thanks for stopping by you two, but you'd better be on your way. Go have fun." She made a shooing motion with her hands.

"All right, we're going." Jared leaned over to give her another hug, and when he was done she opened her arms to Madison.

"You take care of him, okay?" she whispered.

A cold ball of lead thudded into her stomach. "Sure will."

They drove in silence for a while. Then Jared turned on the radio and the mood lightened.

"What kind of music do you like?"

"All kinds. Soft rock, pop, country, jazz."

"You like jazz? Great." He pressed a preset button and lively saxophone music filled the car. She snuck a sideways glance at him. He wore a dark t-shirt and faded blue jeans. He looked like he belonged in a soap commercial. Smelled like it, too. She fiddled with her purse strap.

She needed to get a grip. Imagine him with pock marks all over his face, and a beer belly. Perform some kind of cleansing to get him out of her system. She frowned. No detox diet would get rid of this.

He tapped the steering wheel with his thumb in time to the music and glanced at her. "What's the matter?"

Heat rose to her face. She couldn't tell him she was hoping he'd suddenly become unattractive to her. "Nothing." She plastered on a smile. "Why do you think your dad bought us tickets to the zoo?"

"I don't know. He and Irene were acting funny."

They sure were. The way they kept exchanging glances, like they shared some little secret. And Irene's smile held a message she couldn't decipher. "Yes. They're definitely up to something."

The hour passed quickly, and soon they were in line to enter the zoo. The day hadn't yet turned hot, and a pleasant breeze fanned them. "I've never been here," Madison admitted. "I'm looking forward to it."

Jared turned to her, a half-grin on his face. "You know, I used to come here with my parents when I was little. I couldn't say Henry Doorly, and my parents got a kick out of me requesting to go to the Hunky Doorey Zoo."

Madison laughed. "That's cute."

His face grew serious. "Then my mother died, and we stopped coming."

She slipped her hand in his without thinking, then regretted the intimate gesture, but couldn't remove it without drawing attention, so she left it. "Maybe today will bring back some good memories."

"Maybe."

They got through the gate and studied the map. All of the attractions looked good. Madison wasn't sure which to start with. "What do you want to see first?"

He glanced around. "This place has changed a lot since I was a kid. They've built a bunch of new buildings."

"Ooh, look. There's one called Kingdoms of the Night. It sounds interesting."

"Sure." He squeezed her hand and shivers coursed up her arm, which she tried to ignore.

Kingdoms of the Night turned out to be a wonderfully fabricated cave with exhibits showing bats, snakes, scorpions, and other such creatures. The lower level took you through a dark swamp with water containing beavers and alligators. It was a little spooky, and Madison found herself clinging to Jared's arm, and immensely enjoying the experience.

Jared couldn't deny the feelings invading him as he walked through the exhibits with Madison. His pulse raced with every touch. She grew more excited with each display, pointing to the little creatures scurrying under the brush, and leaning over to see the animals swimming in the dark. She hid nothing. Most people he knew wore masks. Madison's personality didn't seem to allow it.

"Let's go to the jungle next." Her smile lit up her eyes.

They toured the Lied Jungle, Madison reaching out from the suspension bridge to touch the waterfall, and squealing when the monkeys jumped from one vine to the next. He glanced down at the ring on her finger, the one he'd given her, and a part of him wished it wasn't pretend.

After the jungle, Madison pulled him over to another map. "Let's ride the train!"

She looked so happy, he didn't have the heart to tell her it was probably for little kids, and they'd be sitting with their knees up to their chins. "Okay. I think we can buy tickets over here."

While they waited in line, he heard someone call to Madison.

"Madison Nichols? Is that you?" A young woman tugging a two-year-old behind her approached them. A casually dressed man followed them, his hands in his pockets. The woman's hair was pulled back in a French knot, a pair of designer sunglasses on top of her head.

Madison's expression turned wary. "Debbie?"

"Madison, I haven't seen you in ages." Her sneer belied her words. "I told Derrick that was you, but he didn't believe me. You remember Derrick from high school, right? Captain of the football team." The woman indicated the man, ignoring the child now looking up at Madison with large blue eyes.

Derrick gave Madison a half-wave.

"How's the acting career coming along?" Debbie peered down her nose. "Last I knew, you'd moved to California."

Madison's cheeks tinged pink. "I'm...uh, taking a break from the acting right now."

The urge to protect Madison overcame Jared, and he put his arm around her shoulders.

"Oh, you poor dear. Couldn't make it in Hollywood, huh?" She clicked her tongue. "Well, Derrick here just got a position at Hartford and Harrison, the law firm in Bellevue." She patted her husband's arm, a gloating smile on her face.

Jared couldn't stand it anymore. He stuck his hand out. "Nice to meet you, Debbie. I'm Jared Jameson, Madison's fiancé."

Debbie's gaze traveled the length of him, her expression changing. "Oh."

That shut her up, and Jared hid a smile. He picked up Madison's hand, turning it in such a way so Debbie could see the rock on her finger. "In fact, the wedding is coming up soon."

Debbie's eyes grew large as she noticed the diamond. She glanced from Jared, to the ring, and back to Jared. "I think I've heard your name before. What do you do?"

"I'm the CEO of Jameson Technologies, in Crimson Ridge."

"Oh." She couldn't seem to be able to think of any other stinging comments to toss at Madison. The child, apparently bored with standing there, tugged on Debbie's hand. "Baa baa."

For the first time, Debbie glanced down at the child. "Yes, we'll go see the goats in a second. Mommy's talking." Then she rolled her eyes.

"He's a darling." Madison smiled down at him.

"Baa baa," he said again.

Debbie ignored him. "He doesn't talk yet."

For the first time, Derrick spoke. "We've been looking into enrolling Eli in a program."

Debbie huffed and shot a glare at her husband. "He doesn't need a *special program*." Her voice held such distain. "He's fine. He'll talk when he's ready." She threw her nose in the air. "Nice to see you again, Madison, darling. You have a great wedding." She squeezed Madison's arm, then trotted off, trailing her son and husband behind her.

Jared watched them leave. "An old friend?" he asked, sarcastically.

"Yeah, right. She tortured me all through school. Why'd she even come over and talk to me? She never did in high school."

"She wanted to gloat. Throw her husband's success up in your face." A knot formed in his stomach. "She's inconsequential."

A grateful smile crossed her face. "Thanks for the fib."

They were at the front of the line for train tickets now, so he couldn't respond. He purchased them, and they walked over to the train tracks to wait in another line.

The seats on the train were cozy, but thankfully not so small that he was uncomfortable. He didn't mind being forced to sit close to Madison. When the breeze blew in his direction, he smelled the light flowery scent of her perfume. She laughed in delight when the train jerked and began down the track.

After the train ride, they caught the IMAX movie, a beautiful film about the plains Indians who had populated the area years ago. The cinematography was gorgeous, with zooming shots taken from a helicopter of the Nebraska flatlands and lazy rivers.

The rest of their time at the zoo went quickly as they rushed to see as many exhibits as they could. When it grew late and it was about to close, they realized they'd only made it half-way through. "We'll have to come back and finish the rest sometime," he said, before thinking it through.

Her face glowed as she slipped into the passenger seat. "I'd like that."

He shut her door and frowned. What did he just do? Ask her out on a date? He got in the driver's side and started the car. Was he on a date right now?

He drove back to his parent's house, his thoughts swirling around in his head, getting muddled up with his feelings for Madison. Tomorrow he'd be back at work. Madison would be off job hunting. He'd be able to think more clearly. That's what he needed. To get away from her and have a clear head again. Then he'd be able to concentrate on something other than the way her hair shined in the sun, or the way her smile reached her eyes.

15

Madison was silent on the drive home. She'd failed miserably. What happened to getting him out of her system? Wasn't she supposed to convince herself he was unattractive and not right for her? What was she thinking today?

The time spent with Jared at the zoo had been delightful. All thoughts about being careful had flown from her head, and she had let herself go. And she'd gotten closer to the edge of the cliff. She had to stop before she found herself crashing to earth in a tailspin.

When they walked in the door, Irene was there to meet them. She wore a black satin evening gown and heels.

"Wow, you look nice, Irene. Are you going somewhere?"

"No." Irene's smile seemed suspicious. "How was your day?"

She didn't want her sour mood to spoil the thoughtful gift Irene and Maxwell had given them, so she pasted on a grin. "It was wonderful. I think I liked the cave creatures the best."

Jared chuckled. "Even though you clung to me the entire time?"

"It was a little creepy. But fun." She flashed another smile at Irene.

Irene raised her eyebrows. "I'm glad you had fun. Your special dinner awaits."

Jared's face paled. "Um, did you cook for us, Irene?" His voice cracked.

She waved her hand. "Oh, I didn't have time to cook today. But I'm not ruining the surprise. You'll each find an outfit in your room. Change and get ready, and I'll come get you."

As they climbed the stairs, Jared leaned over and whispered, "What do you think that's all about?"

Madison shrugged.

They entered the guest bedroom and Madison gasped. An exquisite royal purple gown hung on the back of the bathroom door. Sequins dotted the fabric, making it shimmer in the light. Matching shoes lay on the floor.

She turned to see Jared holding up a tux, one eyebrow raised. "Did you know about this?"

"No. I don't know what's going on." She couldn't complain, though. The dress was gorgeous! She snatched it from the hanger and went into the bathroom to change.

When she emerged and her gaze fell on Jared, her mouth dropped open. The tux fit him perfectly, accentuating his broad shoulders and trim waist. His dark hair fell forward, and his grey eyes pierced through her. He stared at her, took a step toward her like he wanted to take her in his arms, but he hesitated. He stuffed his hands in his pockets and cleared his throat. "You...you look nice."

She twirled, letting the silky fabric flow out, then brush against her legs. "Thank you. This is a beautiful dress. I wonder where Irene got it."

His eyes didn't leave her. "I haven't seen it before."

"And how did they get a tux that fit you so perfectly? It looks tailor made."

His lip twitched. "It is. I wore this to my father's last three weddings."

"And you left it here?"

"Seemed like the best place for it. I'll probably need it again next year."

Madison was about to tell him what she'd noticed about Irene and his father when a knock sounded. "You two love birds ready?" Irene's muffled voice came through the door.

"Yes," Jared said, his gaze still on her.

Irene opened the door and ushered them down the hallway. "Come on, things are set up out back."

Jared placed his hand on her lower back, and heat seared her skin, sending tingles through her. She tried to ignore it.

Irene opened the sliding glass door, and Madison almost gasped. The backyard was decorated with hundreds of twinkling lights. Several citronella candles flickered in the breeze. A wooden canopy stretched over a table decorated with white linen and two place settings. Maxwell stood by the table. He was in a tux as well. As they approached, he pulled out a chair and motioned for Madison to have a seat.

One side of Jared's mouth curled up. "What's all this?"

His father pushed her chair in. "We thought you deserved a quiet, romantic evening. You've been under a lot of stress. The circumstances have to be difficult for both of you."

Jared didn't say anything, he simply nodded and took his seat.

"We've got appetizers coming in a few minutes. Irene planned the menu," Maxwell said, leaning over. "But I convinced her to use a caterer."

A full smile spread on Jared's face. "Thanks."

"Enjoy your wine." He motioned to the two glasses already filled with a dark liquid. Then he bowed and left them alone.

Madison glanced around. "Wow. This is amazing."

"I'm stunned."

She lifted her glass and took a sip. Her emotions swelled. "Your father and Irene spent a lot of time on this."

A look flashed across his face, and his gaze intensified. "Yes."

She fiddled with the napkin on her lap. If Irene had wanted them to have a romantic dinner, she'd pegged it. Not only was the setting perfect, but Jared looked amazing in his tuxedo. Her heart fluttered.

He continued to stare at her, like he wanted to say something but couldn't bring himself to. Then the patio door opened and Irene stepped out. "Here's your appetizers." She placed a tray in the middle of the table. Grilled shrimp with lemon sauce, and freshly baked bread.

"This looks delicious, Irene. Thank you." Madison grinned.

"You're welcome." Irene folded her hands in front of her. "How would you each like your steak?"

"Medium rare," they said at the same time.

The tinkling of Irene's laugh filled the air. "You got it." She skittered off, leaving them alone again.

Madison bit into a shrimp, and the burst of flavor practically made her moan. Perfectly cooked, the juice filled her mouth as she chewed. "These are delicious."

Jared nodded and popped another one in his mouth. "I hope we're using these guys for the wedding."

They ate in silence, the air sizzling between them. Madison's heart pounded so loudly, she feared he would hear it. She folded her hands in her lap and tried to regulate her breathing.

Maxwell appeared next with a tray of plates. "Your salad, steak and potatoes." He set the dishes down and left as quickly as Irene had.

Jared picked up his utensils and cut his meat. He threw her another meaningful stare, but this time he spoke. "When did you start getting into astrology?"

"When I was an early teen. I find it fascinating that the celestial circumstances surrounding your birth can have so much impact on what kind of a person you are."

A contemplative look crossed Jared's face. "What do you mean?"

"Take my mother for example. Of course, free will comes into play, but my mother has everything stacked against her. She was born under the Scorpio sun, with Leo rising, and Pisces moon, and Neptune on the ascendant. It was obvious to me why she got involved in the party lifestyle."

He slowly nodded. "I see."

"It really helped me understand her more, you know?" Madison took a bite of her baked potato.

His gaze had turned intense again. "You had blamed yourself, and learning about astrology helped you remove that blame."

A tightness started in her throat and spread into her chest. "Maybe you're right. Who wouldn't blame themselves? On my sixth birthday, my mom showed up, out of the blue. Hadn't seen her in months. I opened the door and she scooped me up and let out this yell like she was the happiest person on earth. I thought she'd come to celebrate my birthday."

He raised an eyebrow. "She hadn't?"

Madison twisted her napkin. "No. She didn't even remember it was my birthday. Gave me a half-eaten pack of gum for a present and started crying, saying she would have bought something nice but she had no money.

"Grandma was hesitant to give her any, so dear old mom swore and threw my cherry chip birthday cake on the floor. The one grandma had spent all morning making. Then grandma caved and gave her what she wanted, the wad of cash she kept in a jar in the top cabinet. Mom left. I watched her through the window. She hopped into a little blue hunk of junk with some guy and he drove off. She'd left him waiting in the car. I guess she knew it wouldn't take long." She blinked back the tears welling in her eyes. She hadn't told anyone about that day, until now.

Jared's jaw muscles clenched. "I know it may not seem like it, but it's a good thing she's not in your life anymore."

She smoothed out her napkin, which had become a mangled mess. "You're right."

After dinner, Irene brought out dessert, which was the best New-York-style cheesecake Madison had ever tasted. Then music started up from a hidden sound system.

The side of Jared's mouth quirked in a cute half-grin. "I think they want us to dance." He stood and held out his hand.

Madison's legs wobbled. "I think this wine is making me feel a little woozy."

Jared didn't comment. He pulled her into his arms and began swaying to the music. The strength of his muscles and the heat of his body mixed with his intoxicating scent played havoc with her heart, and it pounded against her ribcage.

She needed to get away from this man. Get her head on straight. This was not a good situation. She couldn't even think with him nibbling on her ear.

"Stop it," she whispered.

"They might be watching us." His breath was hot on her cheek.

"Too bad. No kissing. I mean it." She couldn't take any more of it. One more kiss, and she knew she'd never recover without severe heartbreak. If she could stop this now, she might stand a chance of getting away without too much pain.

Luckily, Jared seemed to understand, because he stopped pressing his lips against her skin. He even loosened his grip on her, putting some space between them.

"Are we leaving in the morning?" Her attempt to make the question light and conversational didn't work. She sounded strained.

His shoulders stiffened. "Yes."

"Good. I have to get back to my job search."

He nodded, his lips tightening. "We'll leave first thing."

16

After thanking Irene and Maxwell profusely, Madison sprinted up the stairs and rushed into the bathroom to take off the evening gown. The way it made her feel was dangerous. She brushed her teeth and got ready for bed.

Jared sat on the bed, staring at his cell phone and shaking his head.

"What's up?"

"I have fifteen voice messages from Veronica." He pushed a few buttons and held the phone up to his ear.

Nerves tumbled in her stomach. "What's she saying?"

"She came by while we were out. She's not happy I didn't get the money to her." He pressed a button and listened again. "She said she was giving me ten minutes to call her back."

"When was that?"

Jared shrugged. "Over an hour ago. Wait, now she says she's going to call Aunt Shelly in thirty seconds if she doesn't hear from me."

Madison dug her nails into her hands. Had she already called?

Jared's eyes grew wide. "Now she wants to forget about the money. She's begging me to take her back."

Relief flooded through Madison. She was right. Veronica didn't want to talk to Shelly. She just wanted the money. "Man, what a psycho."

Jared tossed his phone onto the dresser. "You got that right. To be safe, let's get up early and hit the road. That way, if she comes around looking for me, I'll be gone."

"Sounds like a good idea."

Maxwell shut the bedroom door and slipped his arm around his wife. "You think that worked?"

Irene looked up at him, splaying her hands across his chest. "I think it worked perfectly. But they're insisting on leaving in the morning. I don't know if they've had enough time to realize their feelings for each other."

He blew out a breath, his chest heavy. "That's what I'm afraid of."

A wide grin appeared on Irene's face. "We could send them on a honeymoon after the ceremony."

He laughed and kissed her on the nose. "Perfect."

She tapped her finger on her chin. "Somewhere romantic. Maybe, Hawaii?"

Irene knew how to give the gift of romance. Maxwell pulled her closer, smelling the strawberry scent of her hair. "I'll call first thing tomorrow."

"Did you take care of Veronica?"

"Called her and told her we all know. She hung up on me."

Irene giggled. "Good. Oh, I have a wicked idea."

He nuzzled her neck. "What?"

"We could make a few arrangements. Pay the fake pastor to get an online license. We could make this wedding real."

He pulled back, shocked at the suggestion. "We couldn't do that." He knew they were in love, but forcing a real marriage would be pushing it too far.

Irene ran her fingers through his hair. "They're in love. We know it. Shelly knows it. They just don't know it yet."

"We need to help them realize it. Not trick them into something."

"In less than two weeks, Madison is going to walk down an aisle, stand in front of everyone in a beautiful white dress, and say 'I do' to the man she loves."

"So?"

"She's going to be wishing it were real," Irene whispered.

The intensity of Irene's gaze startled him. "But Jared—"

"He's been holding his relationships at arm's length for so long, he doesn't know how to pull closer. This wedding will affect him, too. He'll come away from this with a different attitude. And he'll want Madison even more."

He wavered. She had a point. Standing before your family, saying the words, exchanging rings, it all gives a person a different perspective. He should know. He'd done it enough times. But the minute he met Irene, he knew she would be the last. Something about her made him feel complete. Like he'd been walking around with a chunk of him missing since Lilly died. Irene filled that missing piece. And he could see it in Jared's eyes. He felt the same about Madison.

"Maybe…"

"I knew you'd see it my way." Her laughter filled the quiet room.

⸻

Jared pulled the car up to Madison's apartment, his chest tightening. "Well, I guess I'll see you next week."

"When's the rehearsal?"

"Next Thursday. Irene wants us to stick around and help out with last-minute wedding plans on Friday, and Saturday's the big day, so you'll want to pack for a few days."

"Okay."

Her large blue eyes stared at him, and he almost forgot what else he wanted to say. "I'll call you. We'll make arrangements." Part of him was relieved to say goodbye and put some space between them. Another part, the part he didn't understand, wanted to cling to her.

Madison didn't look like she had any issues with him leaving. "Okay. See ya." She waved and hopped out of the car. Moments later, she sprinted up the stairs and entered her apartment without so much as a glance back.

And that was it. She was gone.

He tried to feel relief. Told himself he'd be able to concentrate on his work now. He put his car in reverse and backed out. Now he could forget all about her. His life could go back to the way it was before. There was just one thing preventing normalcy.

He had to marry her first.

Pretend to marry, of course. It wasn't real. She didn't love him, and he...well, he wasn't sure how he felt anymore. Her close proximity these past few days had messed with his head. And now things were all mixed up.

Did he love her?

A car honked and he slammed on the breaks to avoid a collision. He waved an apology, while the other driver made a rude gesture. "Sorry." It was pointless saying it out loud, but he did it anyway.

Madison stirred up things he hadn't felt in a long time, but that didn't mean he loved her. He'd had feelings for Veronica, too. What a messed-up situation that had turned out to be.

Getting away from Madison was the best thing for him. He'd go back to work and forget all about her. At least, until he had to say 'I do.'

How he'd gotten mixed up in this crazy scheme, he'd never know.

⚶

Madison ran up the stairs to her apartment, putting as much distance between her and Jared as she could.

Finally.

She could breathe and not smell him, not be reminded every second how attractive he was. She opened the door to her apartment and saw Carrie huddled on the couch, a blanket pulled over her shoulders and mascara streaks down her face. A pile of crumpled tissues lay scattered on the carpet. Her long, black hair obviously needed a good washing, as it was matted and stuck out in all directions.

Madison sunk to the floor beside her long-time friend. "What happened?"

Carrie pulled a tissue out from under the blanket and dabbed at her eyes. "Trevor dumped me."

"Oh, honey, I'm so sorry." The words were true, even though Madison disliked Trevor. She never wanted to see Carrie upset.

"I don't know what happened." Carrie sniffed. "Everything was going well. I mean, we had our moments, like every couple, but I really thought he was the one."

Madison had to bite her tongue so she didn't say something she'd later regret. Trevor was as self-centered as they come. He never did anything for Carrie. Everything had to be his way. Instead of pointing out all of Trevor's faults, Madison concentrated on consoling Carrie. She patted her shoulder. "I know you did."

"He broke up with me in a text. Can you believe it? A stupid text message. He's found someone else. Someone he likes better." A large tear rolled down her cheek.

The words 'good riddance' stuck in Madison's throat, and she coughed into her fist. "That's awful."

"I'll never find anyone else." Carrie yanked another tissue from the box on the floor and blew her nose.

"That's not true." Madison had seen this happen a dozen times. Always the same cycle. Carrie was the type of person who couldn't be without a boyfriend. Within a week of a breakup, she would have a new guy on her arm.

Not that she didn't take her relationships seriously. She did. Maybe to a fault. Every guy was 'the one,' and she clung to him until he couldn't breathe. At least that's how it looked to Madison. But she'd never say anything to Carrie. It would hurt her feelings.

"Do we have any ice cream?"

"You don't need ice cream. You need to get up off the couch, take a shower, and take your life back." Inspiration struck. "Hey, we need to go shopping and find you the perfect dress to wear to my wedding." Madison wiggled her eyebrows.

"Your wedding isn't even real," Carrie moaned and pulled the covers over her head.

"No, but there will be real men there. Jared's half-brother is cute."

Carrie peeked an eye out. "Really?"

Ha, she knew it. Mention another man, and Carrie would snap out of her depression like a twig in the desert sun. "He's not only cute, he's in his last year of law school."

"Ooh, a handsome lawyer?" The covers flew off and Carrie stood. "What are we waiting for? We've got a killer dress to shop for."

"That's the spirit."

17

Madison wrapped herself up in job searching and helping Carrie forget about Trevor. They spent the next day shopping and getting their hair done. Carrie got a trendy bob, and Madison sprung for some highlights. The busier she kept, the less she was plagued with thoughts of Jared. Before she knew it, the day before the rehearsal dinner arrived.

Nerves tangled up inside her as she waited to hear from Jared. When the phone rang, she jumped. Carrie answered, then tossed it to Madison. "Your fake fiancé wants to talk to you."

She tried to make her voice sound nonchalant. "Hey." Her fingers gripped the phone so tightly her knuckles turned white.

"The rehearsal starts at one tomorrow."

That was Jared. Down to business. No asking how she was doing, how her week was going. Nothing but the necessities. Of course, why would he ask about her week? He didn't care. She knew he didn't love her, but the truth of it still stung. "Okay."

"We should leave in the morning. How does eight o'clock sound?"

The deep timbre of his voice brought back all the memories of their time together, which made her heart thump in her chest. Heat rushed to her cheeks. "Sounds good."

Carrie stared at her from across the room. She turned and walked away to avoid the scrutiny.

"Is everything set up with your actor friend?"

"Yes. Jimmy's ready." Madison twisted a lock of her hair around her finger. She didn't want their conversation to end. She hated to admit it, but she missed talking to him. "Did you speak with Veronica?"

Jared blew out a breath. "Yes. She's groveling, trying to take everything back. She wants to date after our fake breakup. I told her to jump in the lake."

Madison giggled. "You didn't!"

His chuckle sent shivers through her. "Yeah. Only I wasn't that nice."

"I hope she leaves you alone now."

There was a rustling noise as Jared adjusted the phone. "What else can she do?"

Madison bit her lip. "I don't know, but she makes me nervous."

"I won't let her do anything to you." His voice was soft, like a caress.

Why did he have to say that? Madison closed her eyes, unable to respond. His words almost made her think he had feelings for her. Pain stabbed through her, because she knew he didn't.

"I'll see you tomorrow." The way he said it meant he was done with the call, back to the business side of things.

"Okay. Bye." Madison hung up and slumped into the living room chair.

Carrie pointed an accusing finger in her direction. "Ha! I can't believe it. You like him."

Great. This was the last thing Madison needed. If Carrie found out, she wouldn't let it go. The best course of action was denial. "I do not."

A raised eyebrow told her Carrie wasn't buying it. "Look at you. You're flushed and shaking. You should have seen your face when you were talking to him. You not only like this guy, you *like* like him."

"I was nervous."

Carrie snorted. "You were nervous because you have the hots for him. Come on, I thought this was just another acting job for you. What happened? Spill it."

Apparently Carrie wasn't going to let up. Madison sighed. "Okay, I sort of fell for the guy."

"Sort of? When you were on the phone, you had huge moonie eyes, and now you're moping. You fell hard."

"All right. I did. But he doesn't feel the same way, so I'm out of luck. End of story."

Carrie put her arm around Madison's shoulders. "Aw, sweetie, are you sure?"

"Yes." Wait, was she sure? "No. I mean, I don't know. Things got all muddled up when I was with him."

"Then we must find out."

Madison picked at a piece of lint on her t-shirt. "How?"

"I'm your bridesmaid. Irene practically begged me to stay at the house after the rehearsal dinner. Don't worry. After seeing the two of you together for a couple of days, I'll know. The Carrie love radar is never wrong."

Madison bit back her response. The Carrie love radar had been in desperate need of repair for quite some time. But instead of commenting, she nodded.

Carrie squeezed her shoulders. "Things have a way of working out in the end."

True. They did.

Just not always how Madison wanted them to.

Madison woke at four in the morning and couldn't fall back asleep. Every time she closed her eyes, Jared's face came into view. Her chest constricted. Was it possible he had feelings for her? She didn't want to let the hope settle in, or she'd be even more devastated when things didn't work out.

An hour later, she finally gave up trying to sleep and hopped out of bed. She opened her closet and pulled out the cute skirt and top she'd found on sale. It was embarrassing to admit she had bought them to look good for Jared.

After a hot shower, she dressed and pulled her hair back in an up-do. She took longer than usual applying her makeup. Normally, jewelry wasn't her thing, but she put on a set of silver bangle bracelets that accentuated her engagement ring. A pair of new leather sandals completed the look.

Carrie whistled. "You look good, girl. If he wasn't interested before, he will be now."

Heat rushed to Madison's cheeks. "Thanks."

While Carrie took her turn in the bathroom, Madison packed for the weekend. She'd bought a couple of other outfits, splurging and spending more than she'd planned. After writing Carrie a rent check, she barely had enough to make it another few days. Next week would be a ramen noodle and peanut butter sandwich week. It would also be after the wedding, when she would have no more excuses to see Jared. She didn't want to think about next week.

She tossed another shirt and a pair of shorts into her bag, zipped it shut, and declared her packing done. The clock told her she still had over an hour before Jared would be there.

Feeling anxious, she logged onto her laptop. It crawled at a snail's pace. Luckily, she wasn't in a hurry. She checked her email, then noticed a couple of new friend requests on Facebook. She clicked the first one. Irene Jameson. And the second one was Mark Jameson. Her blood froze.

Of course Jared's family would friend her on Facebook. That made total sense. But she couldn't accept them. Her status said 'single.' She and Jared weren't even Facebook friends. Her updates said nothing about getting married.

Her heart sank to her toes. How was she going to handle that one? She bit her lip, contemplating changing her status to 'in a relationship.' No one would notice, right? Who would care if she wasn't single anymore?

She searched for Jared Jameson. Quite a few popped up, but none of them were right. Maybe Jared didn't use Facebook. That would solve some of the issues. She felt relief until she saw his photo near the bottom of the list. Great.

A quick friend request sent to Jared, and she closed the computer. Once they were friends, she would add Mark and Irene. Hopefully, they wouldn't ask about the lack of wedding stuff on her wall or pay attention to the fact that she'd only just added Jared as a friend.

A knock on the door startled her. Jared was early. Her pulse raced and nerves shot through

her. She wiped her hand on her skirt before opening the door.

Seeing Jared sent her heart into overdrive. He
wore a green polo shirt with tan slacks. He
looked good. Real good. Her instincts were telling her to run to him, wrap her arms around
him, and bask in the warmth of his embrace. But
they weren't a couple, and there was no one
around to put on a show for. Hugging him would
be inappropriate, so she took a step back and
swallowed the lump forming in her throat. "Hey.
Carrie's still getting ready. Come on in."

Jared's gaze traveled over her. "You look
nice."

Her cheeks heated. "Thanks."

The air tingled between them. Jared sat on
the couch, on the edge of the cushion like he was
waiting for his first date and had to make small
talk with her father. Madison sat next to him
and fiddled with her fingers in her lap.

"What did you tell your roommate?" He
looked worried.

"She knows everything. But she's cool. She
won't tell anyone."

He wiped the back of his neck. "That's good."

"How's Shelly?"

A frown creased his brow. "Still having breathing problems. None of the tests have shown anything conclusive. It's frustrating."

Madison wanted to put her arm around him. To pull him close and console him. Instead, she put her hand on his leg. "I hope they find out what's wrong soon."

"Yeah. Me too."

Carrie entered the room and Madison withdrew her hand like she'd been caught sticking it in the cookie jar. Carrie threw her a knowing look, then smiled. "I'm ready."

They piled into Jared's car, Carrie quickly taking the back seat so Madison was forced to sit in front. As soon as they were on the road, Carrie rested her arms on the backs of the seats and stuck her head between them. "So, Jared, what's it like planning a pretend wedding?"

He shifted. "Pretty much like you'd imagine."

"Fun?"

"Awkward."

"Oh." Carrie's face fell. "But there's something a little magical about a wedding, don't you think? Something that makes you want to fall in love?"

Madison shot Carrie a dirty look. What was she trying to do? She said she'd watch him, not grill him.

"Never really thought about it," Jared mumbled.

Carrie leaned forward. "I mean, doesn't it almost seem like fate is bringing you and Madison together?"

Madison gave Carrie the 'shut up now' signal, which was basically a murderous stare.

Jared raised an eyebrow. "What are you trying to say, Carrie?"

Her 'I'm going to kill you' look must have gotten through to Carrie because she slumped back in her seat. "Nothing. I just think you two make a cute couple."

⌒≈⌒

Jared squirmed, heat rising to his face. Even Carrie could see his attraction for Madison. He chanced a glance beside him. Madison sat rigidly, a look of sheer terror on her face.

Great. If the thought of them being a real couple garnered that kind of a reaction, he should give up now. She obviously disliked the idea.

"Is Mark dating anyone?" Madison asked, changing the subject.

"Not that I know of." Jared eyed her, suspicion growing in him. "Why?"

She tossed her hair over her shoulder. "No reason."

Perfect. She's interested in Mark. He sighed and flipped on the radio.

Carrie leaned forward. "I wanted to know. She asked because of me."

"Oh."

This week away from Madison had been the longest week of his life. He'd tried to go back to his old life. Jump both feet into the way things were and forget about her. But he found his life hollow and lacking. He missed her. The way she laughed with her whole body. Her smile. Her jokes. Even her catty remarks.

Over the last week, he'd pondered the situation. When had he fallen for her? That first night, when she ate Irene's horrible potatoes? Or when she'd conned him into writing the check? Or maybe it was when she trusted him enough to tell him about her horrible family life.

He wasn't sure how it happened, but he knew he couldn't walk away from her after this. He had to show her he cared. Convince her to give him a chance. Maybe they could continue the farce while they dated for real. The thought of continuing to see her made him smile.

But the terrified look she wore at the thought of them being a couple had blown his confidence away in the hot August wind. She wasn't interested in him. Her goal was to become a famous Hollywood actress, which he was sure she'd achieve. Why would she want to date him? He'd only pull her down and tie her to a small Midwestern town with nothing to offer.

She sat in the passenger seat, her long legs crossed, hair pulled back, more beautiful than he'd ever seen her. Their eyes met, and he turned away, embarrassed to be caught ogling.

Tension mounted in him as they drove. Carrie chatted in the back, thankfully. Otherwise, he and Madison would have sat silent the entire way. He nodded and made approving noises where appropriate.

They pulled into the curved drive and parked, his stomach tied in so many knots a sailor would be proud. The day was promising to be another hot one. He grabbed the luggage from the trunk.

As Irene welcomed them into the house, Madison slipped her arm through his, effortlessly easing back into her role of fiancée. It seemed so natural for her. Another knot formed.

Irene played the perfect hostess. "So nice to meet you, Carrie. Let me take your things. Follow me up the stairs, and I'll show you to your room."

Jared jogged up the steps behind everyone and set the luggage on the floor of their guest bedroom. He wasn't sure how, but he needed to find out if Madison was interested in pursuing a relationship after the wedding was over. What an awkward conversation that would be. 'Hey, after we're married, do you want to go on a date?'

He shook his head. No. Maybe he could show her he cared over the next couple of days. Maybe she would really fall in love with him.

Yeah right. Like that would really happen.

18

Madison found it easier than she thought to reclaim the role of being Jared's fiancée. She cozied up to him at lunch and slipped her hand into his when they went out back to admire Irene's setup for the wedding. Jared responded warmly, even kissing her on the forehead when they were standing on the stage where the dancing would take place.

Irene had transformed the backyard into the perfect setting. A beautiful white runner lay on the ceremony path. The twinkle lights still hung from every branch.

Others began arriving: first Pastor Ryan, then Mark, Zach and Patricia, and finally Jimmy. Dressed as he was in full ministerial attire complete with black robe and white collar, Madison worried Jimmy was over-doing it. She soon relaxed, though, when everyone accepted him as the real deal.

They sat in the living room chatting, staying inside where it was cool as long as they could. Patricia and Zach sat on the love seat, clasping hands. Patricia's face practically glowed. If Zach was nervous, he didn't show it.

Carrie managed to sit by Mark, and flirted ruthlessly. Madison figured they'd be a couple by tomorrow. Carrie usually hooked the guy she wanted, the one exception being the handsome teller at Wells Fargo who, they found out later, had a boyfriend.

Pastor Ryan reminded Madison of George Clooney. She could imagine him breaking a lot of hearts in his younger years. He leaned forward and cleared his throat. "Before we walk through the ceremony, I'd like to take a few minutes, if that's okay." He glanced at Jimmy, who seemed oblivious. When the pastor didn't get a non-verbal go-ahead, he said, "Pastor James?"

Jimmy started and glanced around the room. "Who, me? Yeah, sure, go ahead." He waved his hand.

Pastor Ryan nodded. "I'm so thrilled you've invited me to be a part of this happy occasion. Patricia, Jared, I've known you both since you were small. You are like family to me. And this is why I must be bold and say this." He paused and looked them in the eye. "Marriage is not to be taken lightly."

Madison's stomach dropped. Guilt flooded through her, and Jared's face drained of color.

"Not to say that a couple needs to date for years before they tie the knot. I firmly believe when you know it's the right person, there's no reason to delay. In fact, I've always felt putting off marriage and family isn't good. But I want to impress upon you the importance of what you're doing here on Saturday." His gaze pierced through Madison, and her soul shrunk back like a child caught drawing on the bedroom wall.

"Marriage is a commitment. You will stand before God and pledge to love, honor and obey for the rest of your lives. I expect you all to take the commitment seriously."

Everyone nodded, and Patricia wiped a tear from her eye. "Yes, we do take it very seriously, Pastor."

"I know you do. And you'll be happy for years to come, I'm sure of it." His face relaxed into a smile. "Pastor James, anything you'd like to add?"

Jimmy stood. His baby-smooth skin and gangly appendages made him look like a teenager. "Yes, thank you, Father...I mean, Pastor. I just wanted to say that marriage..." His gaze bounced around the room, and he fidgeted, shifting his weight from one foot to the other. "Marriage is what brings us together today."

Jimmy rocked back on his heels while the room sat in silence. Madison tossed Jared a feeble smile. Jimmy continued. "Marriage...that blessed arrangement. That dream within a dream." He appeared to be getting into the role, because he raised his hands dramatically. "You should treasure your love. True love will follow you forever."

He made a dramatic flourish with his hands, and sat down. Everyone nodded, apparently satisfied with Jimmy's words of wisdom. Madison wondered what she'd been thinking, hiring him to play the part.

"Then I'll give a short speech, you'll exchange vows and rings, I'll pronounce you man and wife, then you will kiss your bride. Why don't you practice the kissing part?" Jimmy wiggled his eyebrows.

Jared suppressed a smile. Kiss her? He'd love to. But she'd pronounced the 'no kissing' rule last week, and he didn't want to do anything against her wishes. He stared at Madison, searching her blue eyes for silent permission. When she inched toward him and raised her chin, he took it as assent, and he pulled her close, wrapping his arms around her slender waist. With as much self-control as he could muster, he grazed her soft lips.

The feel of her skin and the light flowery scent of her perfume pushed his heart into overdrive. Sparks ignited under his skin, sending tingles through him. She responded by entwining her fingers in his hair, drawing him closer. She seemed like she was into the kiss, but was it just an act?

Unsure when the 'no kissing' rule would be put back into place, he decided to take advantage of the moment, figuring he might not have another chance to show her his deepening feelings. When they parted, he swung her around in a dramatic dip, his arm supporting her back. She let out a surprised squeal, but the corners of her mouth lifted in a smile. He pressed his lips to hers again, this time more passionately. The crowd hooted and clapped, and when the kiss ended, she laughed—the kind that came from her toes and warmed his heart.

His father shot Irene a look he couldn't comprehend, and she smiled in response. Patricia giggled like a fifth grader. Jimmy stared at them with a half-grin on his face.

"Okay," Pastor Ryan said as he stood. "That will conclude the ceremonies."

Irene clapped. "Thank you Pastor Ryan, Pastor James. Since the August heat has decided to grace us, we'll eat indoors. Fortunately, the weather forecast for Saturday looks to be much cooler."

After the rehearsal dinner, when things had settled down and everyone lounged around in the living room area, Madison excused herself to use the powder room. Jared had acted the perfect gentleman the entire evening. Played the part of fiancé, holding her hand and gazing lovingly into her eyes. The more the evening progressed, the more she found herself getting wrapped up in the act, almost able to believe their love was real.

But it wasn't, and she needed to get her head on straight. She turned on the faucet and splashed her face. The water combined with the frigid air conditioning caused her to shiver. She grabbed a soft towel and patted dry.

Just two more days. That was it. Then she'd be able to go on with her life. If she couldn't find a job here, maybe she should go back to waitressing in California. Surely there was a restaurant that would hire her. She'd only been fired from a few of them. Plenty more to try.

She was headed down the hallway when the locked door caught her attention. Not meaning to snoop but fraught with curiosity, she wiggled the handle once more. Still locked. Maybe if she crouched down and peeked into the keyhole, she could figure out what was inside.

There wasn't much she could make out. A little bit of light filtered in from somewhere, casting shadows of objects she could only guess at.

A flash of blue, and a spot of green, and something gold in the far corner.

"What are you doing?"

Jared's deep voice startled her, and she jumped back, tripped over her own feet and landed on her rump. "Oh! Um, nothing." Heat rushed through her in a full body blush.

Jared reached down and helped her up, the corners of his mouth twitching. "Peek in keyholes often?"

Her face inflamed, she let out a nervous giggle. "No. It's just, uh, curious, is all."

"See anything?" Jared shoved his hands in his pockets and was obviously enjoying her embarrassment.

"Not really. A few splashes of color."

The playfulness vanished from his face. "Good. Doors are locked for a reason." He turned and started down the stairs.

"Wait."

Jared stopped and faced her.

Madison twisted her hands. "I didn't mean to pry. I'm sorry. You don't have to tell me what's in there."

For a moment, Madison thought he was going to come back up the stairs, but he shrugged and said, "Okay," turning back.

"I mean," she said, forcing him to stay. "I really want to know. But if it's private, I understand. It's not like we're really getting married or anything. You don't have to tell me your private things."

He sighed and trudged up the steps again, but the twitching of his lip betrayed him. "It's just my mom's old studio. All that's in there are some dusty paintings." He reached up to the top of the door frame and produced a key, which he used to unlock the door. With a flick of the switch, the room illuminated.

In a room not much larger than a walk-in closet, Madison was surprised to find a desk, chair and easel along one wall. The rest of the room contained stacks of canvas, frames, and paintings in various stages of completion. A large painting of a field of wildflowers hung on the wall. Madison sucked in a breath. "That's gorgeous. Why isn't it hung where people can see it?"

Jared stared at it, clenching his jaw. Then he shrugged. "Dad doesn't like to be reminded of her."

Madison flipped through a few paintings leaning up against the wall. "These are really good. Your mother had exceptional talent. It's a shame to keep these locked up in a stuffy room where no one can see them."

Again he shrugged, but said nothing.

As she continued to look through the artwork, the feeling of the paintings began to change. They grew darker, more foreboding. Happy scenes with sunshine turned to macabre still lives. Broken bits of glass with doll heads lying on the floor, their eyes bleeding. A dark grave-yard, bony hands reaching out of the ground. A small child, his lifeless body floating in a sea of dark water. The last painting had been slashed with a knife until the picture was unrecogniza-ble.

Jared glanced down at the haunting images and turned away. "We should go."

The tone of his voice chilled her. Madison pushed the paintings back in position and fol-lowed him out of the room.

19

Madison slipped between the cool sheets and rested her head on the pillow. The sound of running water came from the bathroom as Jared prepared for bed. His quilt lay on the floor.

The disturbing images of his mother's paintings floated around in her mind. Why would she go from creating such beautiful scenes to painting eerie and disconcerting pictures? And why would she ruin a painting by slashing it? Unanswered questions about his mother plagued her.

The water turned off, and Jared opened the bathroom door. He crossed the room and got situated on the floor. "Good night."

She switched the light off and lay for a few minutes in the dark. The sound of intermediate rustling divulged Jared's restlessness. She bit her lip, unsure if she should voice what was running through her head. Finally, she couldn't stand it anymore. She needed to know. "How did your mom die?" she asked, her voice soft.

Jared sighed. "I figured you'd start asking questions."

When he didn't say anything else, she rolled over on her side and peered at him in the dark. She could just make out his features. He lay on his back, his arms beneath his head, staring at the ceiling.

"Did she...?" The unfinished question was left hanging in the air.

Another sigh. "She struggled with mental illness the last year of her life. No one knows what happened, why it started. She was fine, and then one day...she wasn't fine anymore."

Madison waited for him to say more, but the silence stretched between them. Rather than push, she let him take his time. Finally he spoke, his voice thick with emotion. "The paintings were the first sign that something wasn't right. She became obsessed with death. Then the paranoia set in. She wouldn't go see a doctor."

A lump formed in Madison's throat. Dealing with her own mother's erratic behavior, she knew what it was like. Her stomach tightened. "I'm sorry. That must have been so hard."

"I was only five. I didn't understand what was going on. All I knew was that my mom wasn't acting like she used to. Dad's words were sharper, filled with tension. And Mom didn't want to hug me anymore."

The pain Madison felt as a child, unwanted by her own mother, came back to her in a rush of emotion. She remembered curling up on her bed and crying herself to sleep because her mother had promised she'd come back and tuck her in, only to be disappointed once again. Her eyes stung, and she blinked away the moisture.

"She spent more and more time in her art studio, attacking the canvas with her brush. I went to see her one day after school, and I found her sitting on the floor, red paint dripping from her face and arms. I screamed. I thought it was blood."

Madison clutched the blanket. "I'm sure that was scary."

His voice turned soft. "Then one day, Mom left and didn't come back. They found her car by the lake... and her body at the bottom."

Madison sucked in a breath. "How awful."

"I thought she was mad at me. That if I would just be a good boy, she'd come home. Then Dad brought home a replacement mom, and I knew she was never coming back."

The pain in his voice broke Madison's heart, and tears spilled down her cheeks. She slipped out of bed, climbed under his blanket and put her arm around his chest. "It wasn't your fault."

Jared pulled her close, and she nuzzled his neck. His fingers brushed against her cheek and jerked away at the moisture. Then he cradled her face and his thumb wiped away her tears. "Don't cry for me, Maddie girl," he whispered.

She squeezed him and buried her face in his chest, savoring the musky smell of him. He took a deep breath and let it out slowly, patting her back.

Warmth enveloped her, and she knew. She had jumped off the cliff. But instead of crashing to the earth, she soared above the clouds in a rush of emotion. And as she drifted off to sleep, she gave up trying to save her heart, because it was no longer hers. Jared held it firmly in his hands.

⁂

Madison awoke wrapped in a warm cocoon, and her eyes flew open wide. She'd fallen asleep next to Jared. He lay with his arm tucked around her waist. She wormed her way out from his grasp. He didn't wake, and she snuck into the bathroom to shower.

Emotions surged through her. She'd spent the night in Jared's arms, and even though the floor was hard and cold, she'd slept in blissful peace. Her heart hammered in her chest as she squeezed the shampoo from the bottle.

Last night she'd surrendered her heart to him. She had nothing left to hold back. The feeling both excited and terrified her. Jared could crush her, dash her to pieces by simply saying goodbye. But it was too late to stop her descent. She'd fallen for him, and with an aching in her chest, she realized she loved him.

Apprehension filled her as she stepped out of the shower. The unknown future hung before her, foreboding. Jared's actions toward her were inconsistent. He seemed aloof one minute, and passionately kissed her the next. Of course, the kisses were a show for his relatives. But there was something deeper there. At least she felt it. Maybe she was the only one.

Madison wasn't sure what the day held. Irene had been cryptic. 'Help with the last-minute setup,' whatever that meant. She didn't know what else there was to do. The flowers wouldn't arrive until tomorrow morning. Everything else appeared to be done.

She finished up in the bathroom, then crept around the bedroom so as to not wake Jared, who still lay on the floor. The bed hadn't been used much, so straightening the covers only took a second. She tucked her pajamas into her laundry bag and shoved it into her overnight case.

Jared's cell lay on the dresser. She peered at him, his chest rising and falling in slow rhythm. He wouldn't care if she peeked at her horoscope, would he? She picked up his phone and called up the app.

You feel wound up and restless. People find you tense and excitable. Channel this energy into a useful activity instead of letting yourself be a victim of circumstance. Allow yourself to express your emotions to those you love.

Yeah, right. If she expressed her emotions to Jared, he'd run away, screaming.

"Sleep well?"

His voice startled her, and she whipped around, hiding the phone behind her back. "Stop doing that."

Jared raised his head and rested it on his hand, his elbow on the floor. "Stop what?"

"Sneaking up on me. It's rude."

His eyes held a smile. "I didn't sneak. Someone was making noise and woke me up."

"Sorry."

"You don't sound very sorry."

She slipped his phone in her pocket and sat down on the bed. "What do you want, a card? And in answer to your question, I slept very well, thank you."

His upper lip twitched. "So did I."

A warm blush spread over her. "You'd better get ready. Irene keeps saying we have a full day ahead of us."

"Yeah, I know." His lips spread into a real smile, and his eyes held a secretive gleam.

"Wait, you know something. What's going on today?"

"I'm not saying a word." He mimicked zipping his lips and locking them, then tossed the make-believe key over his shoulder.

Madison laughed. "Fine. I'll go find out from Irene." She pulled on her sandals. When Jared turned his head, she put the phone back on the dresser and headed down the stairs. Something caused her to pause for a moment at the locked door. It was a shame they kept the lovely paintings hidden away. Maybe someday the pain would lessen to a point where Jared could hang them up and enjoy their beauty.

Irene and Carrie were sitting at the island when Madison walked in. "Good morning."

Carrie studied Madison, an eyebrow raised. "Good morning."

Irene wore her long black hair twisted in a knot at the base of her skull, and a floral blouse and skirt made her look too dressed-up for working in the backyard. "I'm glad you're up. We'll be leaving in a half hour. Don't eat a heavy breakfast."

Lifting a cup of coffee to her lips, Carrie hid a smile. She appeared to be a little dressed-up, too, forgoing her normal jeans for a yellow sundress. At least Madison had worn one of her new tops and a pair of nicer shorts that flared out like a skirt.

True to her word, Irene loaded them in the car a half hour later. Carrie chatted happily in the back seat, asking questions about Mark and making it obvious she had her sights set on him. Irene turned out to be a wealth of information. Mark had been seriously dating a woman the previous year, but they'd broken up. He would be graduating from law school next fall, and he was in the top of his class.

Irene pulled into a parking lot. A cute Victorian-style restaurant sat with a large sign proclaiming The Attic Tea Room. As they parked, Patricia got out of a red convertible, along with two other girls.

Patricia squealed and she ran up to Madison. "Can you believe it? The wedding is tomorrow. I'm simply beside myself. Oh, this is Angela and Casey, my bridesmaids. This is Madison, Jared's fiancée."

The girls swarmed around Patricia like bees, humming with excitement. They were skinny and good-looking, with gorgeous tans...the kind of girls who were popular and whose social calendars were always filled. Casey, the taller one, ignored Madison, while Angela peered at her with open curiosity.

Madison introduced Carrie, then eyed Irene pulling out several shopping bags filled with presents. "What are those?"

Irene smiled. "This is your surprise bridal shower, actually, a double bridal shower. You and Patricia are our honored brides today."

A bridal shower? For her? Madison swallowed the lump forming in her throat. Patricia squealed some more and hugged everyone, then dabbed at her eyes. "What a wonderful surprise."

Everyone helped Irene bring the packages inside the restaurant. The host led them to a private room, decked out in white and gold balloons to match their wedding colors. The white tablecloth and gold-rimmed glasses added a sophisticated air to the decorations. They piled the gifts on a table against the wall.

They ate mini muffins, fruit, and breakfast quiche, and chatted about the wedding. Then they played Bridal Bingo and Wedding Trivia. It felt good to be part of a family. But, at the same time, guilt for her deception wormed its way into her stomach. She shoved the feeling aside.

"Now for the best part." Irene stood and made her way across the room. "Present time!"

Apprehension filled Madison. The gifts at the last bridal shower she'd attended had been one skimpy, lacy piece of lingerie after another. Her cheeks heated as she opened the first gift, from Irene. She pulled out a book and prayed it wasn't anything embarrassing.

"Twelve Steps to a Happy Marriage." Madison smiled as relief flooded through her. "Thank you, Irene. What a thoughtful gift."

Next came a set of monogrammed towels from Casey, and a silver picture frame from Angela. The acceptance she felt from these relative strangers made her throat tighten. She didn't deserve this kind of treatment. She was an imposter. She swallowed the bad taste in her mouth.

Carrie's gift came next. A personalized photo album for the wedding pictures. Carrie grinned at her. "So you can open this up and remember your wedding day forever."

Madison knew the underlying message: 'At least you'll have photos of Jared.' The problem was, Carrie didn't know how far Madison had fallen. And how empty her life would be, holding on to an album filled with pretend promises.

Madison shoved the thoughts away and cleared her throat. If she wanted to be an actress, then she'd better start acting. "Thank you, Carrie."

"This next gift is from Shelly. Even though she couldn't be here today, she wants you to know how happy she is to have you joining our family."

Madison blinked away the moisture gathering in her eyes. The package contained a red silk robe and a lacy teddy for underneath. The girls giggled and hooted. Madison was filled with too much emotion to be embarrassed.

After they got home, Madison excused herself and curled up on the guest bed. Thirty minutes later, Jared entered the room.

"You okay?"

The concern in his voice pierced her soul, and pushed her over the edge. This wasn't right. She couldn't do this anymore. "No, I'm not okay. I can't go through with this."

"What do you mean?"

Madison wiped the tears from her cheeks. "I can't do this. The wedding is off."

20

Jared stared at Madison in disbelief. "Wait, what?" She couldn't call the wedding off. It would devastate his aunt.

Tears streamed down her face. "What are we doing, Jared?"

Confusion muddled his thoughts. She'd been fine this morning. Happy, even. Now she was hysterical. "What's wrong? Did something happen at the bridal shower?" He sat next to her on the bed.

Her eyes narrowed. "You didn't answer my question. What are we doing here? Are we really going to pretend to get married tomorrow?"

Jared looked up at his tuxedo hanging on the back of the bathroom door. He bit back the urge to shake her and yell, "Well, duh!" Something told him that would be the wrong thing to do. Instead, he patted her shoulder. "What happened, Madison?"

"Nothing happened!" She sniffed. "We just can't do this."

That made no sense. Of course, women often made no sense. It was probably hormones. The bane of every man's existence. He'd rather scrub toilets than deal with PMS. A whole pile of toilets. He sighed. "Yes, we can do this. It's only one day. You put on a dress and smile. That's it. It will all be over on Sunday."

That must have been the wrong thing to say because she stared at him, a stunned look on her face. Then more tears flowed. She rolled over, away from him. "I can't do it. I'm sorry. I have to leave." She got off the bed, unzipped her duffle bag and began stuffing clothes in it.

Jared glanced longingly at the toilet. The springs on the bed groaned as he stood. He crossed the room and took her shoulders in his hands to calm her, and stop her from packing. "My aunt is very sick. She may not live much longer. Shelly's last wish is to see me married. If we don't go through with this, she'll be devastated."

She peered up at him and blinked. "I don't want to hurt Shelly."

"I know." He rubbed her arms. "You care about her. I can see that."

She stared at the floor. "I never wanted to hurt anyone."

He pulled her close. "Of course not."

"And I was just fine until everyone was so nice to me. And Shelly, she was too sick to come, but she gave me this bridal shower gift anyway and welcomed me to the family, and Irene was sitting there smiling with tears in her eyes, and everyone smiled at me, and I felt awful, Jared, simply awful."

Jared didn't know how to respond to her. It sounded like a garbled mess of female craziness to him. But he wasn't about to admit that. "There, there." He patted her back.

"I don't know how I can go through with this." Her voice sounded thin, hollow.

He tightened his arms around her. "If we call this thing off, Shelly will be so disappointed. You need to think of her."

Madison took a shaky breath and let it out slowly. "You're right, of course. I'm not thinking clearly."

He nodded, then decided agreeing with her that she wasn't thinking clearly was not the best idea, so he masked the gesture by looking around. "It's only one more day."

A silence settled in the room. Neither of them spoke for a few minutes. Finally she pulled away from him. "Just one more day. Then what?"

The question seemed to hold weight, and as she stared at him expectantly, he had no idea what the right answer was. The selfish side of him wanted to keep seeing her. He wanted to say, "Then we'll date each other because I like you." But she'd just spent forty minutes crying, and the only reason he could figure was because his family had been nice to her. The last thing he wanted was to start that again. So, he shrugged and said, "Then you're off the hook."

She stared at him, slowly nodding. "Off the hook," she mumbled.

He couldn't tell if that made her happy or not, but she wasn't crying, so he went with it.

"Yep. Off the hook." To emphasize how great it would be, he grinned like a stupid Cheshire cat.

She nodded again, went into the bathroom and closed the door. The rest of the day seemed to go smoothly. At least she didn't cry anymore. But around dinner time, he realized she'd been avoiding him. He couldn't catch her gaze, and she'd gone out of her way to sit between Carrie and Patricia.

She snuck off to bed early, and by the time he realized this, she was snuggled under the covers, asleep. Whatever he'd done wrong this time, he didn't want to know. He just hoped she'd be over it by tomorrow.

⁂

Madison stared at the dress. Her wedding dress. The most beautiful thing she'd ever seen. Too bad looking at it made her want to throw up.

"You have the dress on yet?" Carrie called through the door.

"Just a minute." Madison bit her lip. There was no backing out now. She had to put the thing on and pretend she was a happy bride.

She undressed and slipped the gown on. "Okay, you can come in."

Carrie burst through the door, already in her gold bridesmaid dress and heels, her hair swept up in a formal up-do. "Oooh, you're going to look so good."

Madison blinked back tears.

"Hey," Carrie cooed. "No tears. We talked about this."

A dagger stabbed at Madison's heart. "He can't wait until it's over, Carrie. You should have heard him yesterday. 'Just one more day. That's it. Then you're off the hook.' But that's not the worst part. He was happy it was almost done. He smiled like he'd won the lottery."

"You have a whole day to dazzle him. Use those feminine wiles God gave you. He'll be begging to spend more time with you." Carrie flashed a smile, showing off her white teeth.

Madison let out a breath. Sure, it was easy for Carrie. She flirted and always got the guy. It was eerie, actually. Maybe Carrie had hidden pheromones Madison didn't possess. Some primitive flirt gene that failed to be passed down her family line.

It was easier to agree with Carrie than continue to argue, though, so she nodded. "You're right. I'll dazzle him."

"That's the spirit. Now turn around and let me zip you up. The hairdresser's been waiting for fifteen minutes."

Madison sucked in her emotions and let everyone swarm around her, tugging on her hair, applying makeup, attaching the train to her dress, and finally adding flowers and a veil to her head. Carrie clasped her hands and oohed. "Girl, you look amazing." She turned Madison around to the mirror.

The girl staring back took her breath away. A stunning French twist dotted with little white flowers adorned her head. The dress accentuated her figure, and the veil cascaded down her shoulders and back. Carrie shoved the bridal bouquet into Madison's hands and proclaimed her the perfect bride.

Her stomach clenched, and she gripped the flowers so hard her knuckles turned white. She took a deep breath and repeated *I can do this* until she felt better.

Carrie ushered Madison down the hall and held her train while she descended the stairs. Irene stood in the foyer, also dressed in gold. She gasped and made a fuss over Madison at the bottom of the stairs.

"Look at you. Such a beautiful bride. Jared will be beside himself."

"Thank you, Irene. You look stunning yourself." Madison gave her a quick hug.

Patricia came down the stairs with her bridesmaids, a trio of squeals and giggles. More hugs exchanged, a few 'you look amazing' sentiments, and then Maxwell appeared wearing a sleek tux. His salt and pepper hair gave him a distinguished look.

Since Madison's parents had been 'killed in a car crash,' and Patricia's father had died in the war, Maxwell had volunteered to walk both brides down the aisle. As he held out his elbows to the two brides, Madison's heart swelled. His gaze radiated his love for her. She pushed aside the guilt and took his arm. Today, she would be a part of this family, even if tomorrow ripped her heart out.

The bridesmaids slipped out to get in line for the processional, and she was left with Maxwell and Patricia. Her heart hammered in her chest. She hadn't seen a glimpse of Jared since she awoke, but figured he was in the other room, waiting for the music to start. Irene had insisted they not see each other until she walked down the aisle.

The faint sound of the wedding march carried through the house, and soon Irene poked her head around the corner and motioned for them to come down the hall. As Madison walked beside Maxwell, her throat swelled. This was it. She would walk down the aisle and say "I do" in front of people who loved her. And it was fake.

She imagined a cameraman following them. This was like any other acting job. That's all it was. She would act, play her part, and nothing would go wrong.

They arrived at the sliding-glass door just as the bridesmaids started down the aisle. With the door open, a cool fall breeze entered the house. Flower petals were already sprinkled on the runner, as they had decided not to have a ring bearer or flower girl. Maxwell ushered them through the door. The music swelled, and the crowd turned as they started down the aisle.

Shelly sat in a wheelchair in the front row. Madison swore she looked better than she'd ever seen her. Pink spots of color touched her cheeks, giving her a healthy glow. She wore a bright floral dress, and her smile warmed Madison's heart. Shelly took out a tissue and dabbed at her eyes.

Jimmy and Pastor Ryan stood at the front, with Jared and Zachary waiting for their brides. Madison's gaze connected with Jared's, and her heart dropped to her toes. Not only was he handsome in his tuxedo, but he stared at her with such intensity, she had to look away.

But after she took her place in front of Jimmy, she couldn't avoid his gaze any longer. She looked into his eyes and fell all over again. Her heart would never recover.

A movement from inside the house drew her attention. Veronica emerged through the sliding-glass door, a wicked smile on her face. And then Madison saw who accompanied Veronica. The woman stumbled outside wearing a wrinkled miniskirt and a button-down shirt that stopped short of her navel and appeared to have been sitting in the dirty-laundry pile for more than a few days. Her hair was teased and styled as if she were a performer at a hard-rock concert, and her ankle-boots sported six-inch heels. Her makeup was smeared like she'd slept with it on.

"Baby doll," she cooed as she stumbled up the walkway. "Why didn't you tell me you were getting married?"

Everyone turned to stare, and Madison's blood froze. She tried to speak, but all that choked out was a single word. "Mother?"

21

A sudden rage filled Jared, and an urge to protect Madison. He took a step in front of her. "Veronica, you have no right to be here. Take that woman and leave." Veronica folded her arms and smirked.

Madison's mother staggered closer. "I can't believe my baby is getting married!"

Jared held up his hands. "Sorry, folks, for the interruption. I'll be back in a minute." He stormed down the aisle, grabbed both women by the arm, and dragged them into the house. When he rounded on them, he found Madison had followed him. She slid the door shut.

"Mother, what are you doing here?" For a moment, something changed in Madison's eyes. Vulnerability emerged. The pain from years of abuse crumbled away, and all that was left was a young child yearning for the love of her mother. But then her gaze hardened, and that girl vanished. "You shouldn't have come."

"Baby, I wouldn't miss your wedding day." The woman held her arms out again, but Madison backed away. The smell of booze and cigarette smoke hung on the woman's breath like a thick fog.

Jared moved in between them. "Don't touch her."

Veronica's eyes narrowed. "You can't do that. Annie is her mother. She has a right to be here."

Madison raised her chin. "She signed away all rights to me. I owe her nothing."

And then all three women started shouting at once, Annie insisting on her parental rights, Madison urging her mother to leave, and Veronica demanding they allow Annie to stay.

Jared held up his arms. "Hold it. Everyone be quiet." When he had their attention, he said, "Veronica, you and Annie need to go. Now."

A wicked smile played on Veronica's lips. "I think we can come to some kind of arrangement."

Annie stuck out her bottom lip. "I came all this way, and this is the thanks I get? I don't even have any gas money to go anywhere. Maybe if I had gas money…"

The tears in Madison's eyes were what fueled Jared's anger to the breaking point. How dare her mother come crash the wedding to panhandle? He clenched his fists. "You will leave here now, or I will call the police."

"Whoa, dude, we don't want no police." At the sound of the male voice, everyone turned to see a man standing in the walkway to the kitchen. He wore a leather jacket, and his hair hung in long scraggly waves. "What's taking you guys so long? I thought we were just going to pick up some quick cash and head out."

Madison's cheeks flushed. "Really, Mom? You left your boyfriend in the car while you came to my wedding to hustle the groom? I think that's a new low for you."

Annie instantly melted into tears. "See how she treats me? See what I've got to go through? I have nothing, while you…" Annie pointed an accusing finger at Madison and glanced around the room. "Just look at you. Marrying into *wealth*. While you live in a mansion, I'm lifting seat cushions scrounging for spare change."

"And why is that, Mother? You've never worked a day in your life. All you care about is the next party. The next drink. And you'd do anything to get it."

Annie's tears dried up faster than spit on a summer sidewalk. "How dare you speak to me that way? I gave you life. I'm your mother."

"You may have given me life, but you were never my mother."

Annie picked up a porcelain vase and hurled it at the wall. It broke into several pieces and left a dent. "I sacrificed for you! Do you think I wanted to have a baby? I could have—"

"Stop!" Jared picked up the phone. "I'm calling the police."

Just as he suspected, Annie and her boyfriend paled and took several steps back. Veronica lunged for the phone, which he raised, and her momentum carried her past him. She landed on the glass coffee table, which shattered on impact.

Veronica screamed and jumped up and down, trying to get the tiny shards of glass off her. A thin line of blood appeared on her right hand, and she screamed again when she saw it. "You assaulted me! You threw me into that table! Now I'm bleeding. Did you see it, Annie?" Her wild eyes darted around the room until they connected with their target. Annie backed up even more.

"I don't want no trouble." The man held up his hands and sprinted out of the room, probably to get his stash out of the area before the police showed up.

"Wait, don't leave me!" Annie stumbled after him.

"Traitor!" Veronica screeched. Then she turned to Jared. "You pushed me, and I have the blood to prove it. I'm going to press criminal charges and sue you!"

Madison fisted her hands. "I saw the whole thing. It was your fault. I'm an eye-witness."

Veronica's face turned three shades of red. "It's your word against mine."

A smirk crossed Madison's face. "And their word as well." She pointed to the sliding glass window behind her. Most of the people from the backyard wedding were there, a collage of faces pressed to the glass, over a dozen pairs of eye-balls staring at the scene.

Veronica swore and stormed out.

Madison once again stood under the flowering trellis in front of everyone, staring into Jared's eyes. Jimmy was done with his speech, which was mostly a montage of movie lines about love and honor strung together, and now everyone waited for Jared to recite his wedding vows. Madison hoped he hadn't forgotten to prepare at least a little something.

Jared pulled out a piece of paper, unfolded it, and peered at it. After a moment, he folded it up again and stuffed it into his pocket. "You know, I had something stuffy prepared for this, but at this moment, it doesn't seem to fit. So I think I'll just wing it."

He took her hands in his, the warmth of his skin sending sparks through her.

"Madison, when I first met you, I thought you were a nut case." A smattering of giggles erupted from the audience. "You exasperated me. You said things that made me want to toss you into the wood chipper." More laughter.

Madison shot him a warning glare.

Jared kept his face blank, but his eyes smiled. "But then I got to know you. You're amazingly witty. You think quickly on your feet. You have this way of disarming everyone around you, putting others at ease, and making them like you. And as I spent more time with you, I fell more deeply in love. It's hard to be without you. When I'm not with you, I miss the way your laughter bubbles up from your toes. I even miss your crazy horoscope obsession. Can you believe I checked mine this morning?" He paused while the audience laughed, and she struggled to swallow the lump forming in her throat. "Madison, I promise to love you, honor you, care for you, and be faithful to you from this day forward for the rest of our lives. I want to grow old with you."

For a split second, everything around them melted away, all of the people and wedding decorations vanished, and she was left alone with Jared. For the briefest moment, his words were real, and looking into the depths of his eyes, she could see a man baring his soul, opening himself up to her. In that moment, the love they shared was legitimate, and today was the beginning of the rest of their lives. But then he blinked, and the world came back into view. He was once again just playing a part for his sick aunt. And tears blurred her vision.

The crowd responded with a collective sigh. They'd bought it, hook, line and sinker. And now everyone waited for her to speak.

A sudden anger flared up in her. How could he stand there and tell her those things without meaning them? What kind of cruel joke was this, anyway?

She squared her shoulders. "Jared, our romance has been like nothing I've ever experienced. From the moment you ran into me in the women's bathroom, to the time you tried to tell me you loved me in Spanish, but instead called me a lonely chicken head...I've known you were something special. And now, here we are, on our wedding day, and you confess in front of God and these witnesses, that you once contemplated throwing me into a wood chipper." Laughter floated through the backyard.

"And through it all, even the time you set my apartment on fire trying to cook me a romantic dinner, I've loved you."

She didn't mean for those words to slip out. She was going to make a joke out of her vows, instead of saying her rehearsed part. The vows she truly felt. But once the confession of love came out, she couldn't turn back. She slipped into her practiced lines.

"I love the way your lip twitches when you're trying not to smile. I love the way you protect me from all the ugliness of the world. I love how you believe in me. When you hold me in your arms, it feels like I can do anything. Jared, I promise to share my life with you. All my ups and downs. I promise to love, cherish and honor you, forever more."

A few of the women in the yard sniffed and dabbed at their eyes. Madison stole a glance at Shelly. A bright smile lit up her face, and she exchanged a glance with Irene. Then Jared pulled her attention back to him as he slipped her wedding ring on her finger, and repeated the lines Jimmy said. It fit perfectly with the engagement ring, creating a beautiful swirl of diamonds on each side.

She slid a ring on his finger, her hands shaking, and her voice barely above a whisper as she told him how the ring was a symbol of her love.

Jimmy cleared his throat. "Madison, do you take Jared to be your husband, to live together in the covenant of marriage? Do you promise to love him, comfort him, honor and keep him, in sickness and in health, and, forsaking all others, be faithful to him as long as you both shall live?"

Madison stared at Jared's strong jaw line, chiseled features, and his steel grey eyes. Her heart pounded in her chest. "I do."

Jimmy's voice faded into the background as he spoke the same words to Jared. She stood, waiting breathlessly for Jared to speak. She knew the wedding wasn't real. But she waited for it anyway. When he squeezed her hand and said in a clear, strong voice, "I do," it shattered her heart. How she wished he really did.

22

Jared took Madison's hand and pulled her close, breathing in the smell of her light floral perfume. The sun hung low in the sky, casting long shadows. They began to sway to the music. Patricia and Zachary shared the dance floor with them.

The song was popular and sappy, probably one he'd agreed to while not paying attention. The singer crooned about love lasting forever, and he glanced down at Madison. Her face masked her thoughts.

"What are you thinking about, Mrs. Jameson?" He meant it to be a joke, lighthearted and teasing, however his voice deepened, and it came out more serious than he'd intended.

Her eyes focused on him. "Don't call me that," she snapped. Her lips pressed together in a thin line.

"Sorry. I was just joking."

"It's not funny."

He exhaled slowly. The day had been like a rollercoaster. With her mother showing up uninvited, making a big scene, and Veronica's ugliness, it hadn't started out too well. Then things had gotten better as they made it through the ceremony. When Jimmy said, "You may kiss the bride," he'd given her the kiss of a lifetime. She'd smiled at him afterward, but it hadn't reached her eyes.

She'd seemed happier when she tossed the bouquet, giggling while Carrie tackled Patricia's friends in order to catch it. Through dinner she'd been quiet, more sullen. But when they cut the cake, she'd hammed it up, smearing frosting on his face and getting cake up his nose, her laughter pealing through the air.

Now, she was angry again. If he lived to be a hundred, he'd never understand women.

Her eyes softened. "I'm sorry. I shouldn't be short with you. You've been wonderful today. Thank you for helping me deal with my mother."

He squeezed her hand. "I can't believe she showed up."

"Veronica tracked her down, I'm sure. Promised her who-knows-what to come crash the wedding."

"I think that's the last we'll see of Veronica." Jared laughed as the image of her sprawled out on the floor after shattering the coffee table flitted through his mind.

Madison smiled. "Yeah, I hope so. Maybe the embarrassment of it all will force her to leave town."

"Wouldn't that be nice?"

They danced in silence for the last part of the song, and she seemed to be in a better mood. As soon as the dance ended, Jimmy waved Madison over. She crossed the yard, and Jared searched for an excuse he could use to see her after today.

❦

Madison followed Jimmy down the garden path, to the gazebo. The small pond bubbled, and the bright orange fish darted around under the water. Even though the gazebo had twinkle lights, it wasn't dark enough yet to see them very well.

She glanced around to make sure they were alone. "What is it, Jimmy?"

He cleared his throat and tugged at his collar. "I just wanted to talk to you for a minute."

"Sure. What's up?"

Jimmy studied her face. "I know this is fake, but you and Jared, you're pretty serious, aren't you? I mean, you love him, right?"

Pain stabbed at her chest. Were her feelings that transparent? But nothing was going on between them, no matter how deep her feelings ran. "We're not a couple, if that's what you're asking."

He narrowed his eyes. "You're not? But you look like you're more than friends."

Frustration welled in her. "What's this about, Jimmy? I should be getting back…"

A bead of sweat formed on his brow, and he swiped at it. "It's just that, well, I did something."

Why was he so nervous? She glared at him. "What do you mean, you did something? What did you do?"

He shifted his weight and wouldn't look her in the eye.

"Jimmy?" Her voice rose. "What did you do?"

The buzz of the cicadas and crickets seemed to catch his attention, because he looked everywhere except at her. "It wasn't my idea."

"What wasn't your idea?" If he didn't tell her soon, she would have to beat it out of him.

"Irene said you were in love. And when I saw you—"

"Wait, Irene? When did you talk to Irene?"

His gaze fell to his feet as he shuffled them some more. "She called me."

"When?" Her heart pounded, and she had to resist the urge to shake him. This was not good.

"Last week."

"Why? What did she want?"

He bit his lip. "She found out, okay? She told me she knew about the fake wedding, and that I was an actor."

Panic rose in her, and her throat closed. "What?" she choked. "She couldn't have."

He glanced around, then met her gaze. "She did. She said they all know. Every single one of them."

Oh, no. This was bad. This was really, really bad. "I don't understand. Why did they let us go through with the charade? To make fools of us? Why would they do that?"

Jimmy grabbed her shoulders and forced her to look at him. "Madison, stop. It's okay. They understand why you were pretending. They think you and Jared really are in love, but they know Jared has commitment issues, so they…"

She stared at him, waiting for him to finish. "So they what?"

Jimmy swallowed, making his Adams apple bob. "They wanted me to go online and get ordained as a minister, so the marriage would be real."

As his words sunk in, the garden began to swirl around them. Jimmy's face blurred. He grabbed her once again, but everything went black.

Time stopped for a moment, then someone patted her cheeks. Cicadas roared around her. "Madison, you okay?"

She blinked, and Jimmy's face came into focus. "What happened?"

"You fainted. I…I'm so sorry."

Jimmy looked like he was going to pass out himself. She was about to tell him so, when she remembered what he'd said. Jared's family knew about the fake engagement. And they had schemed with Jimmy to...no. He couldn't have. Could he?

Madison scrambled to her feet. "Jimmy, did you?" Her voice barely came out above a whisper. "Did you go online?"

His eyes widened, and he appeared to be having trouble breathing. "Yeah." He nodded.

She placed her hands on his cheeks. "Are you saying I'm really married to Jared?"

He nodded again.

Warmth radiated over her, and she threw her arms around him, letting out a squeal. "I can't believe it! I'm married to Jared!"

Jimmy stepped back. "You're not angry?"

"Angry? I'm so happy, I could kiss you." She hugged him once more before picking up her skirts and rushing toward the garden gate, her shoes clicking along the stone path. She couldn't wait to tell—

"Wait, is Jared going to be happy about this?"

The question stopped her in her tracks. Would he? Would Jared feel the same about being married as she did? Her thoughts flew back to the vows he spoke. Did he mean them? What if he didn't feel the same?

She turned to Jimmy. "I don't know."

Jimmy stepped off the gazebo and closed the distance between them. "Irene thinks he loves you."

A cold rock formed in her belly. Her stomach lurched. "What if Irene is wrong?"

"I see the way he looks at you."

Hysteria swept through her, and her voice rose in pitch again. "We are acting, Jimmy. He's *supposed* to look at his bride that way!"

Jimmy held out his hands. "Calm down. I'm sorry. I can't undo it. But if it's not what he wants, you can get an annulment."

"Annulment?" The word tasted bitter on her tongue.

"Yeah. It's no big deal. You sign some papers, and it's like the wedding never happened."

The breeze suddenly felt cold, and Madison hugged herself. "All right."

"But you may want to wait to tell him until after I've left." Jimmy rocked back on his heels. "That dude's got some muscles."

Madison nodded, not really paying attention. "Okay."

She wandered back up the path, latched the gate, and crossed the yard. Jared caught her arm. "Where have you been? People are asking for you."

"I was just talking to Jimmy."

"Irene has some kind of announcement. Come on." He pulled her toward the dance floor, where Irene and Maxwell stood with a microphone, like they were about to sing a duet.

The crowd gathered around them, and Irene turned the mic on. "I apologize for this small interruption, but we've got a surprise for the two couples."

Maxwell took the mic. "I know things have been crazy, and the happy couples haven't had time to plan proper honeymoons, so Irene and I have done the planning for them. Our gift to Patricia and Zachary is a trip to romantic Puerto Rico!" He pulled out a pair of plane tickets while Patricia squealed with delight, jumping and hugging her groom.

"And we are sending Jared and Madison on a romantic trip to Hawaii!"

Madison's knees went weak, and Jared caught her before she fell in a heap on the grass. Maxwell handed Jared the tickets as the family members cheered. Shelly beamed.

Irene took the microphone. "While we dance and continue our celebration, we'll let the happy couples take off." Everyone cheered again, while Maxwell jumped off the stage and put his arm around Jared.

"We've packed your luggage, and it's already in the car." He checked his watch. "You'd better change quickly, the plane boards in a couple of hours."

Madison couldn't breathe. How was Jared going to react to this? Being forced to go on a fake honeymoon with her? Well, technically it was a real honeymoon, but he didn't know it. In fact, she was going to have to tell him before they left. It wasn't fair to keep it from him.

Jared took her arm and pulled her toward the house. She peered at him, trying to decide if he was upset or not.

As soon as they were in the guest bedroom, Jared turned to her, the corners of his mouth tugging down. "I'm sorry, I didn't know."

Was he upset? She couldn't tell. He looked more worried than anything. "That's okay," she said, her heart in her throat.

Relief flooded his face. "You don't mind?"

She smiled. "Hmm, spend time vacationing in Hawaii, or go back to my small apartment, broke and looking for a new job?" She tapped her chin with her finger and looked up at the ceiling. "I don't know. I just can't decide."

He laughed, a rare occurrence for him. "Okay. Hawaii it is."

While he changed in the bathroom, she slipped out of her dress and into a casual skirt and top. Her nerves jangled, twisting her stomach into a giant knot. She had to tell him before they left. Right?

Jared came out of the bathroom wearing a pair of tan slacks and a short-sleeved button-down shirt. He could have been on the cover of J Crew. "Shelly looked really good."

"I know, I swear she's improving. Has anyone said anything?"

He shook his head. "No."

"Well, I hope she's on the mend." Madison bit her lip. "Before we go, I need to tell you something."

He raised his eyebrow at her. "Yes?"

Sweat trickled down her back, and she squirmed. What was she going to say? "There's this thing that happened." She made the mistake of looking into his eyes, and the bottom dropped out of her stomach. "You see, I guess Irene did something."

Jared glanced at his watch. "We'd better go. You can tell me in the car." He grabbed her arm and hustled her down the stairs and out the door.

Madison sighed. Yeah, right, like she could really tell him in the car. That way, if the shock of the news made him jerk the wheel, at least they'd be able to honeymoon together in the hospital.

The news could wait until they were standing in line at the airport.

23

Jared heaved the bags of luggage up on the short platform. The woman behind the counter adorned the handles with the white airport stickers. Madison fidgeted with her purse strap. Jared didn't blame her for being nervous. She was taking a trip to Hawaii with someone she'd only met a couple weeks ago. But he was determined to be the perfect gentleman. She needn't worry. He'd get two separate rooms at the hotel, to make her feel at ease.

This would be perfect. Give them time to get to know each other better, while having the stress of family out of the way. They didn't have to act like a couple anymore. And this would give him the perfect chance to see if Madison had any real feelings for him.

"You're all checked in, sir." The woman handed them their boarding passes. "Gate 13, Terminal B. You'd better hurry. You don't have much time."

Jared took Madison's hand and led her down the walkway.

"I really should tell you something before we get on the plane." Madison stepped out of the flow of traffic and pulled him over to the wall. "It's important."

He searched her eyes. "What is it? Do you get air sick?"

She shook her head. "No, nothing like that. It's about Irene...and Jimmy."

Confusion set in. What was she mumbling about Irene and Jimmy? Didn't she know the plane was about to leave? They had to get on, or they'd miss their flight. "Can it hold for a few minutes, while we run to catch our plane?"

She shook her head, and blinked like she was going to cry.

Good heavens. Were her hormones going to be on overdrive this whole trip? He took her hands in his. "Okay, then, tell me."

She drew in a ragged breath, then let it out. Agonizing seconds ticked by. He tried not to look at the clock on the wall. She frowned. "I don't know how to say this."

"Quickly?"

Her face told him that wasn't going to happen. "Irene has this thing. A suspicion or something. She thinks she knows things. Then she acts accordingly."

She kept talking but her words made no sense. Why couldn't she tell him this after they boarded the plane? They still needed to get through security. He waited another minute for her to get to the point, but when she still hadn't told him, he held up his hand. "Stop. Can you tell me while we wait in line up there?"

She blinked, nodded, and then exhaled. "Fine. I'll tell you later."

"Great." He grabbed her hand and tugged her down the path to security.

Madison opened her eyes to sunlight, filtering through the window of her hotel room. Compared to the guest bed at Jared's house, this bed was hard and uncomfortable. Or maybe it was the fact that even though they were married, Jared was sleeping in the other room. She sighed.

She'd tried to tell him, but he hadn't been listening. He'd been too worried about catching the plane. They'd rushed to security, only to be held up by a little old man taking his time waving his wand over people. He must have been a hundred years old. She wasn't sure what he'd do if anyone pushed their way through. Throw his wand at them?

And then once they were on the flight, there hadn't been enough privacy. Their connecting flight had been delayed in California, but they had ended up dozing in uncomfortable airport chairs while they waited. By the time they finally arrived in Honolulu it was the next evening, and they'd been exhausted. When they checked into the hotel, Jared had explained to the man behind the counter they needed two rooms.

He drew his eyebrows together and spoke in broken English. "But you have honeymoon suite, yes?"

Jared nodded. "Yes, but we'd like to change that to two rooms."

The man's gaze bounced between the two of them. "Ah, I see. First quarrel. I give you lover's spat special. Two rooms, one door connecting them." He wiggled his eyebrows up and down.

Jared smiled. "Fine."

As soon as they'd gotten into their rooms, she'd changed and plopped down on the bed, asleep in a few seconds. Now she lay staring at the ceiling, wondering what she was going to do. How strange to think she and Jared were married, and he was in the other room without a clue. A stab of guilt shot through her. She couldn't put it off any longer. She had to tell Jared today. But what if he got mad when he found out the truth?

She rolled out of bed, padded over to the bathroom, and turned on the hot shower. It didn't matter if he got angry. They were married, and she couldn't keep the truth from him. That would be wrong.

The shower invigorated her, made her feel alive and excited to spend the day with Jared. She pushed the thought of telling him away. She'd gauge his mood and tell him when she felt it most appropriate.

As she was fixing her hair, a knock came on the door that adjoined their two rooms. Madison opened it. Jared leaned against the door frame in a casual manner, his arms folded, looking like he'd stepped out of a cologne advertisement. She took a whiff. Yep. Definitely an expensive cologne advertisement.

His muscles bulged under his light button-down shirt, and she had to raise her eyes to his face to keep from staring. His cool grey eyes caught her gaze, and she struggled to breathe. Dang, she had married well.

"Hey," she said, suddenly shy.

His eyes sparkled. "Enjoying your vacation so far?"

She could only nod.

"What would you like to do today?"

"I have no idea. I've never been here before."

Jared pushed himself off the door jamb and took a couple of steps toward her. "There's the memorial at Pearl Harbor."

She wrinkled her nose. "War is depressing."

Jared nodded. "There's a wonderful museum full of Hawaiian history."

"Hmm, isn't there something we can do out-doors?"

He took another step closer. She could feel the heat from his body. If he leaned over, they'd be kissing. His lips twitched. "We're in Hawaii. There's plenty to do outdoors."

"Then let's go spend the day in nature." On impulse, she reached up and mussed up his hair.

"What'd you do that for?"

"You needed a little less 'CEO' and a little more 'I'm on vacation.'"

His hands snaked around her and pulled her to him. "And you need a little 'keep my hands to myself.'"

They stood for a moment, staring into each other's eyes before Jared leaned over and brushed his lips on hers. The kiss was quick and over before she knew it. He let go and stepped back. "Sorry."

"Don't be." And in her mind she said, "We can kiss. We're married." But the words stuck in her throat and wouldn't come out her lips.

24

They ended up spending the day at Manoa Falls, walking the trails and taking countless photos. Madison's heart warmed as she watched Jared loosen up and enjoy the cool breeze and beauty nature provided.

As they ate dinner in a restaurant along the beach, Madison realized it had been a near perfect day. The only problem was the fact Madison hadn't yet told Jared.

Her stomach churned, and nerves tingled in her chest. She couldn't wait any longer. Jared sat across from her, a slight smile on his lips.

He'd never be in a better mood. She needed to spill it, like ripping off a band-aid.

He stood and offered her his hand. "Would you like to walk along the beach with me?"

She nodded. This was it. She took his hand and followed him down the sandy path. The soft waves reflected a calm she didn't feel. Turning to him, she took a deep breath. "I have something to tell you."

His eyebrow raised quizzically. "What is it?"

She looked out over the ocean, the sun painting the perfect backdrop. Best to simply spill it. "We're married. For real."

His eyes widened in surprise. "How is that possible?"

"Jimmy went online and got ordained as a minister."

He picked her up and spun her around. "My dreams have come true."

At least, that's how it happened in her head.

She blinked, realizing he was still standing there, holding out his hand, waiting for her to answer him. "Sure, we can go for a walk on the beach."

She took his hand for real, warmth spreading up her arm. Maybe things would go as she had imagined. Well, he probably wouldn't say the corny 'my dreams have come true' line, but she'd take about anything above him freaking and screaming at her.

The sound of sea gulls carried over the cool evening air. The sunset cast purple and pink hues over the ocean. The faint smell of rain mixed with grilled meat and fresh flowers wafted in the breeze. Jared smiled down at her. "What are your plans when we get back to Crimson Ridge?"

Madison shrugged. She couldn't say, "Move in with you, have a few babies, live forever in marital bliss." So, instead, she said, "Look for a job, I guess." She laughed, but it came out nervous and strained. She wiped her sweaty hands on her jeans.

"I suppose eventually you'll go back to California and give acting another shot, huh?"

She raised an eyebrow. What was he doing? Did he want her to leave? "That's my goal," was all she could say.

Pursuing her acting career hadn't been on her mind lately. But now that he brought it up, she wondered what the future would look like if they did decide to stay married. Would Jared move to California? Or would he expect her to give up her dreams and stay in Crimson Ridge with him?

A silence settled between them, and Jared seemed lost in thought. Now was the time. She couldn't go on without telling him. She gathered up her courage and turned to him. "We need to talk."

They stopped walking and faced each other. He entwined his fingers with hers. A light breeze blew his hair. "Sure. What's on your mind?"

She stared into his eyes. Did she imagine it, or did his gaze hold the same love she felt? She could only hope he took the news well. A deep breath, and she spoke. "Irene found out."

He lifted one eyebrow. "What do you mean?"

"She found out we weren't really engaged. They all did, actually. Your whole family knew." Her heart beat a painful rhythm against her ribcage.

The loving expression melted from his face, and he clenched his jaw. "How do you know?"

"Jimmy told me. Irene called him last week." The next part caught in her throat, but she forced it out. "She asked him to go online and get ordained so the ceremony would be real. He did, and it was."

His eyes hardened, and he stiffened. "What are you saying?"

"We're married, Jared. For real."

He dropped her hand and stepped back like she'd caught on fire. His eyes narrowed. "And you knew?"

This wasn't going as planned. She shook her head. "No. I mean, yes, but I didn't know it when we were going through the ceremony. Jimmy told me after the dance."

Anger poured off him in waves. "And when were you going to tell me?" he shouted.

Madison looked around. Several other couples glanced their way. "Let's not discuss this here," she said in a low voice.

"No, I think this is the perfect place to discuss this. What right did they have to decide something like this? And what right did you have to keep it from me?"

Pain stabbed through her. "I tried to tell you. In the airport."

He pointed an accusing finger at her. "You should have told me right after you found out. At the wedding."

He was right. She should have. She had no defense. "I'm sorry," she whispered, tears falling down her cheeks.

Jared swore under his breath and raked his hand through his hair. Then he rounded on her. "What about you? Aren't you upset?"

At that moment, she knew. She loved him, but he didn't love her back. She'd been happy at the news. His reaction told her everything.

What could she say to him? That she was not upset? She hoped they would live a fairy tale life together? Someday their grandchildren would laugh about the story of how they ended up married to each other?

She struggled to swallow the lump in her throat. She had to say something. Something real. The need to tell him her feelings overwhelmed her. "I hoped we could—"

"We could what? Keep on pretending to be a couple? Pretend to be something we're not to please my family?"

His words cut deep. They were not a couple. He was pretending all along. She blinked back more tears.

He turned on his heel. "I can't stay here," he said as he walked up the beach. "We should never have come. This was a bad idea."

She stumbled after him, fear clutching her throat. "We're leaving?"

He stopped, reached into his back pocket and tossed something at her. "No, you stay. Live it up on Irene's credit card. I don't care. I've got to go back and take care of this mess."

With that he stormed off, Madison watching his retreating back as he faded into the darkness.

25

Jared slammed his car into park and jumped out. He stalked up the walkway, then entered his childhood home. Countless hours on his way home had given him plenty of time to think about what he was going to say to his father. His anger grew every minute that passed. It pulsed inside him.

The door banged shut and he stomped through the house. His father and Irene were sitting on the kitchen stools eating lunch. At the sight of him, they both froze, Irene holding her fork half-way to her mouth, pasta hanging mid-air.

"How dare you?" He narrowed his eyes and clenched his fists, his anger like a fire burning in his chest.

Irene's fork slowly descended to her plate. She cast a worried glance at her husband and licked her lips.

Maxwell blinked. "Jared. Come on in. Sit down."

His casual manner spoke volumes. He didn't care. He'd messed up Jared's life and it didn't even phase him.

"How egotistical and completely typical of you. Thinking you can run my life for me. You've never understood me. Never even cared to try. But this? I can't believe you sunk so low."

Irene's face paled. She glanced around. "Where's Madison?"

Jared ignored her. "I cannot believe the gall you two have. Did you think this would be funny?"

His father stood. "Calm down."

"Calm down? You've gone too far this time. I am *not* going to let this go."

A look of panic crossed Irene's face. "Where's Madison?"

Jared waved her away. "She's still in Hawaii."

Irene clutched her necklace. "What did you do? You just left her in Hawaii?"

Guilt stabbed through Jared. He'd been so mad at his father, he hadn't thought about Madison. But she was a big girl. She could handle herself. "Don't change the subject. Madison's fine." He turned to his father. "What were you thinking? Not everyone treats marriage so lightly. Some people think it means something."

His father hitched up his pants. "And pretending to get married shows how much you think it means?"

"Stop!" Irene hopped off her stool and stood between them. "Everyone needs to cool down."

"No," Jared said between clenched teeth. "I don't need to cool down. I need you to get out of my life." He walked to the archway and turned. "I'm done with you."

◦∾◦

Madison boarded the plane, dragging her carry-on and leaving her dreams behind to die in the fading sun. She'd thought about staying in Hawaii, but couldn't bring herself to do it. It wasn't right to spend Irene's money on a vacation she didn't deserve. She'd lied to everyone. And now the only option was to go back home and bury herself in job hunting.

She plopped down in her seat and stared out the tiny window. For some reason, everything looked smaller through the thick glass, even though the plane hadn't taken off yet. An elderly woman sat down beside her. "Are you okay, miss?"

Madison hadn't realized she was crying. She wiped the tears from her cheeks. "I'm fine."

The woman patted her arm. "You poor dear. What happened?"

What could she tell her? The whole thing was too crazy. In the end, she settled for, "My husband left me."

The woman shook her head. "Well, he must be crazy to do such a thing."

The flight to L.A. took six hours, then she had a long layover and another long flight to Omaha. Luckily, she was able to sleep on the plane, because she had to rent a car and drive for almost four hours to get back to her apartment in Crimson Ridge. When she finally arrived at her apartment, she was emotionally drained and her back ached. All she wanted to do was slip into bed and pull the covers over her head.

She tugged her suitcases up the stairs. The lock stuck, and she had to wiggle her key to get the door open. When she stepped into her apartment, her mouth fell open.

Irene sat on the couch, her arms folded and a concerned expression on her face. She stood, crossed the room, and threw her arms around Madison. "You're home."

Nothing but complete shock registered in Madison's brain. "What are you doing here?"

Carrie and Mark came into the room. Her roommate ran to join the hug. "Oh, Maddie, I'm so sorry." Mark hung back, his hands in his pockets.

"What's going on?"

Irene led Madison to the couch. "Have a seat. We need to talk."

Carrie squeezed Madison's shoulder. "Jimmy told us how happy you were when you found out you were married to Jared."

She swallowed the lump forming in her throat, unable to speak. Everyone knew. They knew she loved Jared and that he didn't feel the same way. A hole opened up in her chest, threatening to swallow her.

Irene dabbed at her eyes with a tissue. "I just can't believe Jared. How could he?"

Fresh tears blurred her vision. "He doesn't love me."

Irene patted her hand. "I think he does. He just doesn't know it yet. You need to tell him how you feel."

Madison stared at Irene. Tell Jared she loved him? What would he say to that? She wasn't sure, but once she admitted her feelings, she couldn't take them back. "I don't know."

"You must be exhausted." Irene picked up a glass of ice water from the coffee table. "Get some rest. Think about it. If you tell Jared how you feel, he might be able to admit his own feelings."

"Or he'd laugh at me," she said under her breath.

Irene gave her a hug. "You won't find out until you do it."

Madison nodded. "Maybe tomorrow. I can't even think right now."

"Of course." Irene stood. "We should go."

"Wait, how's Shelly doing? She looked like she was doing better."

Pink crossed Irene's cheeks. "She's really good. Improving each day."

"Did they find out what was wrong?"

Irene bit her lip, and Mark coughed into his fist. Neither one spoke.

"What?"

A guilty smile crossed Irene's face, and she stared down at the ice water. "Turns out she'd been taking the wrong dose of her heart medication. We, uh, found out soon after she was admitted to the hospital. She was afraid you'd postpone the wedding if she told you...so..." Her voice trailed off.

"I guess we weren't the only ones not being truthful." Madison smiled. "For some reason, that makes me feel a little better."

Mark rocked back on his heels. "Talk to Jared. I think you guys can work this out."

Madison took a deep breath and let it out slowly. "Thanks for coming all the way here, it means a lot to me. But if Jared wants an annulment, I have to go along with it."

Irene cringed. Carrie's face paled.

"I'm just going to have to get past this." Madison stood and hugged Irene again.

After Irene and Mark left, Madison took a long soak in the tub, letting the warmth of the water soothe her wounded soul.

26

Madison swung her car into the parking stall in front of Jameson Technologies and stopped. A feeling of déjà vu overwhelmed her, but this time she wasn't there to beg for a job. She was going to tell Jared how she really felt.

A cold lump formed in her stomach. After thinking about what Irene and Mark had said, she agreed. She needed to talk to Jared. It wasn't fair to keep her feelings a secret.

Her sandals slapped on the tile floor, her long skirt flowing as she strode through the building.

This time she didn't stop at the desk, but entered the elevator and pushed the button to the twenty-third floor. The receptionist called out to her, but the doors were already closing.

When they opened on Jared's floor, Madison walked out and approached Darlene's desk. The woman frowned, the corners of her mouth disappearing into the folds of skin on either side of her face. "Do you have an appointment?"

"No." Madison walked right on past the desk.

"You can't go back there," Darlene yelled, as she ran around her station. But Madison was already to Jared's door. She threw it open and entered his office.

Jared swung around in his chair with his phone to his ear, and his eyes widened. Darlene came up behind her, panting. "I'm sorry, she just barged in."

Jared held up his hand. "It's okay, Darlene."

Huffing, she turned on her heel. Jared spoke into the phone. "Can I call you back?" When he placed the phone down, his steely eyes met her gaze. He didn't say anything, just continued to stare.

"Really? You're still mad at me?" She placed her hands on her hips. What was his problem?

"You did lie to me."

"I tried to tell you. You didn't listen."

He waved his hand, like it wasn't worth his consideration. "Whatever. I'm having my attorney draw up the papers. We'll get an annulment and be done with this whole mess."

Heat flooded her cheeks. That's all this was to him. A mess. Something to clean up. And here she was, ready to tell him she loved him. Like that would happen. "Fine."

She turned to leave, but changed her mind mid-stride. "Listen, you're the one who left me in Hawaii. It's me who should be mad at you."

Jared stood and crossed the room. "If you had told me right away, we could have torn up the marriage certificate. It would have saved us both a lot of trouble."

Anger seethed in her. He was in the wrong. He didn't even apologize. She took a step toward him, now only inches from his face. "You. Left. Me. In. Hawaii." She yelled each word, making sure Darlene could hear. In fact, the people in the next building probably heard.

He narrowed his eyes. "And you lied to me."

That was all he cared about. Getting out of the marriage. All thoughts of telling him she loved him left her, and instinct took over. She clenched her fist and swung, connecting with his eye. Pain shot through her knuckles.

He staggered back, a look of complete shock on his face. She turned and strode out of his office, hoping he didn't see her shake her hand. Darlene and a few other office personnel gaped at her as she passed. The elevator dinged, and as she entered Darlene asked, "Who was that?"

Jared's deep voice answered her. "My wife."

⁓

Jared stared at the elevator doors as they closed, guilt rising in his throat like bile. He deserved that. All he'd been thinking about was himself. How wronged he felt, how manipulated by his father, and how hurt that Madison had kept it a secret. He hadn't treated Madison right. Of course she'd be mad at him. He cursed under his breath.

Darlene glared at him. "You left your wife in Hawaii?" She shook her head and muttered, "I'd have socked you too."

Jared scowled, but didn't say anything. He returned to his office. "Hold my calls."

Darlene snorted. "One more day of holding your calls and I'll quit."

He ignored Darlene and touched his face, wincing when he reached the tender spot under his eye. Yep, that would leave a mark. A chuckle escaped, even though the situation wasn't funny. Madison was sure a spit fire.

Jared stewed for the rest of the day, feeling worse about the situation as the hours sped by. After work, he ran to the gym because he couldn't shake the urge to hit something.

He worked out until his muscles ached and his anger was spent. The hot shower eased his tension, and by the time he'd grabbed a bite to eat and unlocked his front door he was feeling more like himself.

Why did Madison make him so crazy? And why did he have this urge to go to her apartment and grovel until she took him back? They weren't a real couple. The thought was absurd. She'd shown him how she felt today. Going to her would be a bad idea.

A knock on the door startled him. He crossed his living room, which suddenly seemed cold and impersonal with the dark wood and chrome accents. For a bizarre moment, he wondered if Madison had come to apologize, but when he opened the door he found his father.

A look of defeat crossed Maxwell's face, and Jared marveled. He'd never seen his father look so vulnerable.

Jared stepped back, letting him in.

Maxwell squinted. "Is that a black eye?"

"Yeah."

A disapproving frown crossed his father's face. "Bar fighting?"

"No. Madison."

Maxwell's eyes widened. "She hit you?"

He nodded, rubbing the back of his neck. "I guess leaving her in Hawaii wasn't the best idea I ever had."

His father chuckled. "You've got that right." He hitched up his pants and glanced around the room. "I came to apologize."

He actually looked uncomfortable, and Jared wondered if Irene had made him come. "You should."

Maxwell nodded. "You're right."

Jared assessed him. "Why'd you do it?"

"You don't know, do you?"

Was he playing games? "What?"

"She loves you."

Jared scoffed. "Yeah. Thus, the black eye. She can't keep her hands off me."

"She hit you because she loves you. She was hoping you'd find the marriage appealing. Something to celebrate, instead of..." His voice trailed off.

"Instead of upsetting me?" Jared shook his head. "That's crazy. The proof is on my face."

No one spoke for a moment. "Do you love her?"

"What kind of a question is that? I hired her to play a part. She did. That's all there is to it."

"You didn't answer my question."

Frustration welled inside him. "What does that have to do with your apology?"

His father frowned. "You asked me why."

Jared sighed. "You think I love her."

"Don't you?"

He shrugged. His insides were a jumbled mess. He wasn't sure what he felt anymore. Sometimes he did think he loved her. Other times she drove him nuts. "I don't know."

Maxwell patted him on the shoulder. "Then I suggest you figure it out."

After a few minutes of polite chat, his father took off, and he was left to marvel once again at the transformation. Maybe Irene was better for his father than he thought.

Jared scrubbed his hand over his face. The paperwork on his desk blurred, all the numbers running together. He sighed and pushed his chair back, lacing his hands behind his head. This wasn't working.

He'd thought he could get the whole ugly affair out of his mind by jumping back into his work. Forget what his father said, forget he was ever married, forget the whole blasted month of August. Instead, he couldn't stop thinking about Madison. And with thoughts of her came everything else.

Two weeks ago, his attorney had finished the paperwork for the annulment. Everything was done. All he had to do was deliver the papers to Madison. He glared at the manila folder sitting on the corner of his desk. Why couldn't he bring himself to do it? Was his father right? Was he in love with Madison?

When she'd burst into his office, for one wild second he'd thought she was going to tell him she loved him and wanted to stay married. It was a silly thought. And when she yelled at him, he'd realized all she came for was to give him a piece of her mind for leaving her in Hawaii.

Truth be told, it had been callous of him. He'd been feeling guilty, but was too prideful to admit it. He'd let his anger over the situation cloud his judgment. And now he was stuck with the unpleasant task of delivering the annulment papers to Madison.

He swore under his breath and stood up. This was ridiculous. He was a grown man. It was time he started acting like one. Gripping his briefcase, he grabbed the folder and stuffed it under his arm. No time like the present.

Storm clouds hung low in the sky as Jared pulled out of the parking garage and onto the street. By the time he reached Madison's apartment, the heavens had opened up and large drops of rain were falling. He held the folder above his head and sprinted up the walkway.

The rain dripped down his face as he stood outside her door. He pressed the bell and waited as a sudden jangle of nerves tingled inside him.

The door opened and Madison stared at him, her blue eyes wide. Seeing her sent his heart into his throat. Her soft blonde hair was pulled back into a sloppy ponytail, tendrils hanging down around her face. Her full lips parted in surprise, but she recovered quickly. Her gaze traveled over him, then her lips tightened into a thin line. "I figured you'd show up eventually. Come in." She stepped back.

His arm brushed hers when he passed by, causing his pulse to quicken. He stopped in the middle of the living room and stared at her. Why did she always have this effect on him? He couldn't seem to catch his breath.

Her gaze softened. "You're soaking wet." She stalked out of the room, then came back with a bath towel. She patted his face and hair, and the smell of her perfume and laundry detergent enveloped him. Memories flashed through his mind. Time they'd spent together. The times he'd kissed her.

He grabbed her wrist. "I can do that." He took the towel from her and put some space between them.

She folded her arms across her chest.

Guilt tugged at him. "Look, I'm sorry for leaving you in Hawaii. I was just so mad, I wasn't thinking straight."

"You were mad? You left me in Hawaii. Alone. On our honeymoon." Her eyes shot daggers at him.

"It wasn't really—"

"I know. Fake honeymoon. Whatever." She waved it away. "It doesn't matter now." She sighed.

He took a tentative step toward her. Electricity crackled between them. "I know it doesn't mean much now, but I really am sorry."

She nodded. "I'm sorry too. For the...you know." She pointed to his face, and a blush graced her cheeks.

"Yeah, you gave me quite a shiner. It's almost gone now. But I don't think the gossip will die down at the office anytime soon."

A small smile appeared on her perfect lips, but her eyes remained cold. "I guess you came to have me sign something?"

He had, but all he could think about now was the taste of her lips. He pulled his gaze away from her face. "Yes. I have the papers right here."

Madison swallowed. "All right, then." She clasped her hands and stared at the folder tucked under his arm.

Time seemed to slow as he held out the paperwork. She took it but didn't meet his gaze. She left the room, and moments later returned with a pen. "Where do I sign?"

Madison's stomach churned. This was it. Her marriage to Jared was about to be over. She shook her head. What was she thinking? Jared hadn't spoken his vows from his heart, like she had. The marriage was never real.

And yet, a part of her mourned for the loss anyway. Mourned for the kisses that never would be. Mourned that she would never fall asleep in his arms again. The loss weighed heavily on her as Jared pointed and she signed her name.

Jared stuffed the papers back in the file folder and gave her a nod. "Thanks."

He stood for a moment, staring at her, and she gathered up the courage to look him in the eye. For a brief moment, a flash of something crossed his features. Regret? Then it vanished.

A lump formed in her throat. She looked down at the wedding and engagement rings still on her finger. The rings she couldn't bear to take off. She slid them from her finger and extended her hand. His gaze flickered from her hand to her face. Then he took them.

He gave her another nod, pocketed the rings, and turned and opened the front door. He spoke without looking back at her. "We'll have a hearing. I'll let you know when it's scheduled."

And with that, he walked out. Madison let out a breath she didn't realize she was holding. She'd spent the last two weeks trying to convince herself an annulment was for the best. But seeing Jared again made her heart do crazy things. And watching him so callously tossing away their relationship had broken it all over again.

She wiped a tear from her cheek. No use in sitting around crying. She had a job interview tomorrow. Some meat-packing company downtown. The building sat two blocks from Jameson Technologies. Driving past his building would twist the knife a little more each day. Maybe she wouldn't show up for this interview.

Jared sprinted down the steps, the rain coming down in droves, soaking him in seconds. Lightning streaked across the sky, and something crazy popped into his head. Madison once had told him if he danced in the rain, he would find the rhythm of heaven. He looked up at the menacing clouds and couldn't help but laugh.

This was probably not the kind of rain she meant.

He froze. What was he doing? Why was he leaving when all he wanted to do was go back to Madison and confess his love to her?

The thought jarred him. He did love her. He knew it now. He could no longer deny it. His heart ached for her. Every day he thought of nothing else. His life could no longer go on without her beside him. The papers in his hand drew his attention. What if he tore them up? Was that what he wanted?

Yes. The answer came as a clash of thunder sounded. He didn't want to annul the wedding. He wanted Madison. And he was going to go back up there and tell her.

A pounding on the door startled her out of her thoughts. Carrie and Mark were on a date, and she wasn't expecting anyone else. She brushed the moisture from her face and opened the door.

Jared stood there, his fist clenching the paperwork, his mouth in a frown, and rain running down his face in tiny rivers. He shook the papers. "Is this what you want?"

Madison wasn't sure what he was doing back, or why he looked angry. She'd signed them, like he'd asked. Now he wished to know her opinion? Her heart pounded out a quick rhythm. This was it. Her chance to tell him how she really felt.

She slowly shook her head. "No. This isn't what I want." Her words came out in a whisper, and she wasn't sure he heard her over the noise of the rain.

He clenched his jaw. "Me neither." He crossed the balcony and tossed the papers over the edge, the wind and rain snatching them and violently carrying them off in different directions.

Madison gripped the door handle, a flicker of hope growing inside her. "What are you doing?"

Thunder sounded, and he rushed toward her. He took her in his arms out there on the cold and rainy balcony, in a firm grip, and heat seared through her.

"I've been angry for three weeks. Angry at my father, for what he did. Angry at Irene, for going along with it. Angry you didn't tell me. But after my anger settled, I found myself angry this marriage had to end. And I couldn't admit it, but

Irene was right. I didn't want this marriage to just be an accident."

Madison stared at him, unsure if she heard him right.

He continued. "When I spoke my vows, I meant every word. You do make me want to throw you in a wood chipper, but during these weeks we were apart, I missed your laughter. I missed your insane obsession with the stars. I missed you."

He kissed her, his lips moving over hers. The rain pelted them, but Madison didn't care. His kiss was urgent, passionate, and possessive. He trailed kisses along her jaw line, down her neck.

Fire spread through her, and she entwined her fingers in his hair, relishing in the feel of his lips on her skin.

When they parted, she stared into his grey eyes. "I missed you too."

Jared stepped back, then got down on one knee. He took her hand in his. "Madison Nichols, I fell in love with you the first night we met, and every day since that, love has grown. I cannot stand to lose you. Will you stay married to me?"

Her vision blurred, and her heart pounded in her chest. She thought about the life they would have together. The lazy Sunday afternoons and kisses in the night. The pitter patter of little feet as they had children of their own. Growing old together, always being there for each other. The thoughts made her heart soar, and she nodded. "Yes, Jared Jameson, I will stay married to you."

A flash of lightning lit up the sky, and he took her rings from his pocket and slid them back on her finger. Jared stood, a smile cracking his face, little drops of rain clinging to his eyelashes. He brushed her wet cheeks with his thumbs. "I love you, Maddie girl."

Emotions choked her, leaving her without words. She flung her arms around him and kissed him, holding nothing back.

EPILOGUE

Madison tugged her wool coat around her as she started up the walkway toward Jared's childhood home. She looked up at the grey sky. "Is it supposed to snow?"

Jared wrapped his arm around her. "Tomorrow. We should have a white Christmas after all."

Irene answered the door, a festive string of tiny blinking lights around her neck. "Merry Christmas! Come on in. Everyone's in the family room." She held out her arm. "Let me take your coat."

Irene opened the coat closet and turned to Jared. "How was your flight?"

He laced his hands through Madison's, sending sparks up her arm. "It was fine."

"Congratulations on getting the part," Irene said, a sparkle in her eye.

Madison grinned. After Jared convinced her it was no big deal to run his company from L.A., they'd moved out there so she could pursue her acting career. She'd landed an agent and was starting work on a new movie after the holidays. "Thank you. It's a small role, but I have a few speaking lines, and my agent thinks it will lead to other opportunities."

"That's fantastic." Irene squeezed her hand.

They moved into the family room and joined Patricia, Zachary, Maxwell, and Mark, who were already seated. Carrie was arriving tomorrow, as she was spending Christmas Eve with her family. Carrie and Mark had been dating seriously since August, and Madison couldn't be happier for them.

Shelly crossed the room and embraced them both.

"You look good," Jared said.

"And you two, you look happy." Shelly winked.

Patricia ran to Madison. "We've missed you, but I'm so glad your acting career is taking off."

After they were seated, Madison looked around the room at the people she'd come to care deeply for. When her gaze landed on Jared, her heart swelled. If heaven itself had created a man for her, he wouldn't be more perfect. The corners of his mouth lifted in a contented smile, and his steel-grey eyes raked over her. Warmth spread through her.

Maxwell entered the room with a large package. "I have an early gift to give, but it's not from me." He handed the package to Jared. "This is from your wife."

Jared raised an eyebrow at her, and a warm blush touched her cheeks. He tore open the gift, revealing his mother's beautiful wildflower painting, framed and ready for display. He sucked in a breath. Madison prayed he wouldn't get upset.

"I had your father frame this one. I...I thought we could hang it in our living room."

He blinked, obviously struggling with emotions. Then he nodded. "Yes, this belongs on the wall." He set the painting down and stood, pulling her into an embrace. "You're amazing, you know that?"

Everyone oohed while he pulled her close and gave her a toe-curling kiss.

Irene smiled. "Dinner will be ready in a few minutes. Do we want to go to the table?"

Everyone stood, and Jared shot her a look. Luckily, they'd had a large lunch in anticipation of Irene's big Christmas Eve dinner.

Madison tossed him back a knowing smile, and patted her belly. "Good. Then after dinner, Jared and I can share our big announcement."

All eyes landed on them. Patricia squealed. "Really? You're pregnant?"

Madison nodded, a smile taking over her face.

Patricia clasped her hands together, bouncing on her toes. "So am I!"

Zachary's face went white. "You are?"

A blush graced Patricia's cheeks. "I was going to wait to tell everyone, but I can't now. We're going to have a baby!" She turned to Madison. "We should have a double shower."

Jared smiled. "Maddie girl, you sure have a way with announcements." And then he laughed, the sound warming her heart.

The End

ABOUT THE AUTHOR

Victorine and her husband live in Nebraska where they raise their four children. She designs and manufactures rubber stamps for the craft industry, and freelances as a graphic designer. Victorine's first book hit the New York Times best selling eBook list, in March, 2010.

Author's Note:

Thank you for reading this book. I hope you have enjoyed it. As a self-published author, I rely immensely on word of mouth to help spread the news about my books. If you liked this book, please leave a review and tell others. It would make my day! I read each and every review, and I appreciate every one.

Thank you!
Victorine E. Lieske

Find Victorine online at:
www.victorinelieske.com

Email her at:
vicki@victorinelieske.com

Other Novels by Victorine:
Not What She Seems
The Overtaking

Novelettes by Victorine:
The Practice Date
The Truth Comes Out